Fathers Don't Say Goodbye

Eleven Short Stories by Jack Rosenbaum

'

White Knight Studio, Boston

© 2013 Jack Rosenbaum
All Rights Reserved

No part of this book may be reproduced without written permission from the author.

Book and cover design M. Snyder

ISBN: 978-1490415598

Published by White Knight Studio, Boston
For information address: whiteknightstudio.com

Printed in the USA

Contents

Twenty Mile Tomatoes 1

Fathers Don't Say Goodbye 9

Shaving 17

Giver of Gifts 23

Thirteen 35

Nightmare 43

Einstein, Uncertainty, and Ross 49

Ruthie's Pair 59

Court Martial at Sheppard Field 75

The Marcolini Effect 85

Three Stones for Rebecca 99

Twenty Mile Tomatoes

My folks bought the country house on Lake Oscawana in the summer of '46. They were partners in it with my aunt Dorothy and Uncle Gus. I was just out of the Army Air Force and the first time I went up to the house I was looking for a rest, knowing that the war was still too much with me.

The house was made from Putnam Valley fieldstone, with large glass shutters enclosing two sides of an unusually long porch. During July and August the glass shutters were always open, hanging by metal hooks from the porch ceiling beams. Cool breezes carrying the scent of pine, roses, and freshly cut grass sifted through the porch screens and soothed everyone's city-frayed nerves. I fell in love with the place.

And so I came to spend my days selfishly alone on a float on Lake Oscawana, only a few hundred yards from the house. Early in the morning I would pack my lunch and head down to the spring-fed lake. A short walk, a quick splash, a few strokes and I would pull myself out of the cool water onto the canvas-covered float. The July sun was always strong, and while I baked under its heat the quiet of the shrub oak and fir green valley sank into my dusty khaki soul. No hostile Indians came to do battle.

Around five o'clock I would climb the hill heading back to the house. Inside, the kitchen was a scene of intense activity as the women bustled about preparing the evening meal. Aunt Dorothy peeled potatoes while humming to herself. My mother had her hands in a big wooden bowl of chopped meat and raw eggs, which she squeezed through her fingers and let plop back into the bowl. My sixteen year old sister was busy taking down cans from the pantry shelves and opening them on the kitchen table. Grandma Annie was sitting in her wheelchair out on the porch issuing strict orders to my two little cousins who were scurrying about putting forks and knives, napkins and plates in their proper places. Uncle Gus sat in his favorite wicker chair watching baseball flicker in and out on a black and white television screen. Every once in a while he would get up to adjust the metal antenna. My father was the only one missing from the house.

My father was a life insurance salesman and he never stopped working. In the summer he would come down from Albany and work the Putnam County-Duchess County territory. He was successful at what he did and he liked summertime. He especially liked ripe, country-grown tomatoes.

At six o'clock dinner was ready. Everyone was washed clean and sitting around the porch, waiting. Then it came, three loud honks of the Chrysler's horn down at the blind curve in front of old man Haggerty's place. The sound was my father's calling card, announcing to his family and to the world at large that he was home. Home from Peekskill, home from Fishkill, home to where a man could eat a good meal, and rest from selling every farmer and his wife a bushel or a basket of life insurance.

My mother would call out, "That's Murray," and rush to greet him as he huffed and puffed his way up the stone steps leading to the porch. As he entered and the screen door slammed closed behind him, he would plant a large brown paper bag in the center of the dinner table and loudly proclaim to one and all, "Here they are, fresh from the farm, the biggest, the most delicious, the best darn tomatoes I have ever seen!"

My seven year old cousin, knowing what was expected of her, and with a glint in her eye, would coyly ask, "How far did you have to go to get them, uncle?"

My father would look her straight in the face while a crooked grin crept out of the corners of his mouth and spread to the crow's feet at the corners of his eyes.

"Now Barbara, my love, do you believe that your uncle Murray had to travel twenty miles to farmer Brown's place just to get you these tomatoes? Yes, sir, these here tomatoes are twenty-mile tomatoes and we're going to eat them in our salad right now!"

Then everyone sat down at the table and the food was served while little breezes wafted up from the valley and the lake to whisper a summer evening's benediction over the family members gathered together on the porch in the country house.

Before another seven summers had passed into the stillness of memory, my wife and I were bringing our own little boy up to the country house to laze away the days of summer in the cool shallows of Lake Oscawana. In the early evening, close to dinner time, my small son would grow quiet, waiting and listening. Then, suddenly, it came. Three loud honks. David would cry out, "There's Grandpa, I can hear his horn!"

Soon my father would come crashing through the screen door, banging it behind him. In one sweeping motion he would lift David up in his arms, drop the brown paper bag on the table, and whisper into my son's ear with an air of deep mystery, "Tell me, what has Grandpa got in the bag?"

And David would smile up into his grandfather's face as he triumphantly squealed, "Twenty-mile tomatoes! You got twenty-mile tomatoes!"

Over the course of many summers I think each of my three sons and both of my sister's daughters, and even my Cousin Barbara's little girl, were initiated into the summer ritual that always accompanied my father's homecomings.

****

One summer, after the youngest of my boys was five, I went shopping in Peekskill with my father. On the way home, about three miles from the country house, my father swung the car off the road and pulled onto the gravel driveway in front of *TOMMY'S FRUIT AND VEGETABLES* roadside stand.

"Stay in the car," my father said, "I'll only be a minute."

I watched as he went over to a young man who was husking corn into an empty Indian River orange crate. They talked a few moments and then the young man stopped what he had been doing and started putting big red tomatoes into a brown paper bag. When the bag was filled my father put his arm around the young man's shoulders and walked with him back to the car.

He smiled, speaking through the open window, "I want you to meet my friend Tommy here. I guess I've been buying his father's tomatoes now for nine, maybe ten years, ever since he was just a kid."

"Hi," I said.

"Nice to meet you," Tommy answered.

My father got back into the car, depositing the bag of tomatoes on the seat between us. We drove off, leaving Tommy standing in front of his Indian River basket of corn husks.

"Dad?"

"Yes?"

"Are these the twenty-mile tomatoes you've been bringing home all these years?"

"Yep, they sure are."

There wasn't a trace of embarrassment in his voice.

"You lied, you know. You lied to David and Barbara. And you lied to Amy and Suzie and Adam and Danny and all the rest. How could you?"

"Well now, lied is a pretty strong word, isn't it?"

My father stole a glance at me and then concentrated hard on the curving country road.

"Look at it this way. I'm an old, over-the-road salesman. Always have been. I cover forty to forty-five thousand miles of the upstate territory every year. And if there's one thing I've learned it's this. Distance is a relative thing."

"Sure, but what has that got to..." I tried to continue, but my father persisted in finishing his thought.

"Let me explain what I'm getting at. Twenty miles to a man like me is nothing. What is it? Fifteen or twenty minutes more on the road? Hell, the car doesn't get tired. Now, take your mother and your aunt. Are they going to walk the three miles to Tommy's place and the three miles back? Of course not! So it might just as well be twenty miles. See what I mean? And anyway, it makes the lousy tomatoes taste that much sweeter."

I stared at my father's face. He was actually grinning from ear to ear. Suddenly, he turned and winked at me and started laughing. I couldn't help myself. Almost against my will, I joined in his laughter.

****

The summer after I had discovered the secret of the twenty-mile tomatoes I received a long distance call from my aunt Dorothy. She told me that my father had died in his sleep from a massive heart attack and that the funeral would be the following Monday. My wife and I told our sons about their grandfather and then drove up to the country house from the city. Monday morning we drove to the Shrub Oak Cemetery in Adams Corners. How can I describe that day? It was the kind of summer day my father loved for teeing-off in front of the club house lawn. It was cool, clear, and bright with the promise of a warming sun, the kind of sun that sucked up the morning's dew and let a golf ball roll straight to the cup on the green.

The family gathered around the fresh grave and the burial ceremony began. When it was over and the coffin in the ground I looked up and saw Tommy. He was standing next to a gray-haired woman I did not recognize. I walked over to him to thank him for attending my father's funeral. As I approached him he began talking.

"I had to come. Your father meant so much …I mean, he… Oh, this is my mother."

I turned in order to more directly face Tommy's mother. I found myself looking into the palest, most tranquil eyes I had ever seen.

"I'm so sorry," she said. "Please accept my deepest sympathy." She reached out and touched my sleeve. "I believe that what Tommy was trying to tell you is, he was very fond of your father. You must know that your father bought tomatoes from Tommy ever since he was a boy just starting high school, right on through college. I don't know how many times Tommy wanted to give up on going to college and your father talked him out of it. And then, of course, there was that business of the twenty-mile tomatoes. It was kind of a secret pact between them."

"Yes, I know," I said. Then I watched as Tommy's mother's eyes slowly changed expression as she thought of other things.

"Did you know that your father sold my husband a life insurance policy many years ago?"

"No, I didn't," I replied, suspecting there might be more to tell. Then Tommy started talking in a rush to let me know.

"When my father died, Mom used to wait for the mailman to come with those insurance checks from Chicago. She used to say she could not have gotten through the years without them."

"Yes, that's true," said Tommy's mother.

She smiled at me as she said it. I didn't know what more to say. I just stood there looking at the two of them. Strangers. Behind them, I could see two gravediggers at work on that green hill. People were returning to their cars.

"Tommy," I said, "would you like to help me bury my father?"

I put my hand on his shoulder and led him back to my father's grave. I picked up a shovel and threw some dirt down on the coffin. Backing away from the edge of the grave, I handed the shovel to Tommy. He hesitated at first. Then he took it from me, bent, and threw a shovel full of earth down on the man who had invented twenty-mile tomatoes.

Fathers Don't Say Goodbye

Ross could not sleep. He got out of bed and rattled around the old house doing silly things. He flicked on the lights in the different bedrooms and stared mindlessly at the empty beds and unused desks once filled with the clutter of his sons' schoolwork. Then he went downstairs and started emptying ashtrays. He arranged the magazines on the glass coffee table into two neat piles, separating the Smithsonians from the National Geographics. Finally, Ross picked up the phone in the foyer and dialed his son in Boston.

"Hi, Dave."

"Dad, how are you?"

"I'm okay," Ross said. "How are things going?"

"Pretty good, I guess."

"Are they working you hard at the newspaper?"

"You bet, I'm bushed."

"Get a chance to see the game last night?" Ross asked.

"Uh huh, part of it anyway."

"Aren't those Red Sox something? I love to see the Yanks get beat."

"Yeah, I know what you mean. Yastrzemski's pinch hit won it for them."

"Ain't he too much? An old man and he still comes through in the clutch."

"This is probably his last season, y'know," David informed his father.

"Oh, I didn't know that. Too bad. Anything new with you?"

"No, I'm all right. How's Mom?"

"She's fine. We're both doing fine."

"That's good."

"Well, I guess I'll sign off now."

"Okay. Give Mom my love and thanks for calling."

"Sure, I'll give her a big kiss for you."

"Bye now," his son replied.

"You know that's costly!"

Ross looked up at his wife who was standing at the top of the stairs in her nightgown. Her eyes, heavy with sleep, were squinting against the light in the foyer.

"What's costly?" asked Ross.

"Spending all that money to talk to Boston, long distance, and you wind up talking stupid baseball talk with your son."

"We can afford it," Ross replied.

His wife turned away and went back toward the bedroom. From the top of the landing she called down, "Ross, come to bed, it's getting late. I'll never be able to get you up in the morning."

Ross called back, "Please go to bed and don't worry yourself about me. I'll be up soon."

Ross went into the kitchen and poured himself a drink. Then he went into the darkened living room and settled down on the soft cushions of the couch. Light from a street lamp filtered in through the Venetian blinds. Ross stared into the transparent shadows and dimly saw his father's face smiling at him. He shuddered. For years he had not permitted himself to think of his father. Now, in the deep stillness of this late hour, and with his sons' empty rooms overhead, Ross allowed his father's image to enter and fill his mind. He saw the country house, rainy days, and a cold, stainless steel wall.

****

It was summer. Ross and his wife had decided to spend the weekend with his parents at the country house in Putnam Valley. When they left Brooklyn early in the morning, the day was bright with the promise of good swimming in Lake Oscawana. An hour and a half later, when Ross swung the car off the Taconic Parkway at the Shrub Oak exit, a light rain was falling. Unable to enjoy the lake, Ross agreed to go into town with his father and help him get some chores done. His wife and mother remained behind.

Together, Ross and his father took overflowing garbage bags from the kitchen and carried them down the driveway to the steel waste cans by the side of the road. Next, they loaded heavy laundry bags into the trunk of his father's car and drove to the Laundromat at Adams Corners. They sat for a long time watching the clothes go round and round, as white suds sluiced up the porthole window of the Bendix, and checkered sleeves of drowning shirts ducked in and out of the foam. In the adjacent machine white linens sloshed and slid in a tide of Clorox bleach and Ajax detergent. Later, after removing all the laundry from the dryer, Ross helped his father fold the sheets and towels. Finally, they deposited the cumbersome laundry bags in the rear seat of the big Lincoln and took off for Peekskill to pick up his mother's bridgework.

While waiting in the dentist's reception room, Ross' father suddenly threw up his hands in a gesture of futility and said, "Laundry bags and garbage bags, garbage bags and laundry bags, my God, what a way to spend a day in the country!" He looked at Ross and shook his head.

Arriving back at the house, the two men were welcomed by their wives with thick roast beef sandwiches and juicy slices of farm-fresh tomatoes. Ross went to the refrigerator to get some bottles of Pabst Blue Ribbon. His father sat down in the wicker chair on the porch to watch Saturday's televised baseball game. It was rained out.

Sunday morning came with a thick mist that rolled down into Putnam Valley. It clung to the glass panes of the porch shutters and colored the day a watery gray. Ross and his wife decided that it was time to leave Oscawana. They packed their things, said their good-byes, and got in their car. Ross' father came down to the road to stand and wave good-bye. Starting the engine and turning on the windshield wipers, Ross heard the gravel of the road crunch as the car began to move forward. He glanced into the rearview mirror to see his father still standing in the road, waving, even though it had begun to drizzle. As he rounded the sharp curve in front of old man Haggerty's place, his father's reflection disappeared from sight.

Ross was in bed when the phone call came the following Saturday morning. It was his aunt Dorothy. She told him that his father had died in his sleep from a sudden heart attack. The funeral would be on Monday.

"God," Ross whispered to his wife, "I didn't even get a chance to say good-bye."

Ross and his wife gathered their three sons, told them about their grandfather, and helped them put on their best suits and shirts. Soon they were on the road, driving to the country house in Putnam Valley where they always went to spend the precious days of summer.

As the miles raced by, and Sawmill River Parkway turned into Taconic State, Ross kept thinking of the things they had done last weekend. The damned laundry. Why had his father not said something to him ...just to let him know? "My heart is not... what?" And then he thought how incredibly stupid he was being. Does anybody know his own heart? If only he had said good-bye. Saying good-bye to his father seemed very important to him now. The thought nagged at him.

When they arrived at the summer house, the day was bright with the promise of good times on Lake Oscawana. The children of the lake would be splashing out to the canvas covered float. Ross threw open the car door, ran up the driveway and leaped up the stone steps to the porch. The screen door slammed behind him. He desperately wanted to see his father. But his father's body was not in the house. His uncle told him that the law required the county coroner to take his father's body to Community Hospital in Courtland, a town just outside Oscawana.

Ross wasted no time. He hurried back to the car, spun it around, and heard the familiar crunching of gravel under the tires. In twenty minutes he was at the hospital in Courtland. The lady at the reception desk informed him that his father's body was in the morgue in the basement of the building. A male nurse with hairy arms protruding from the short sleeves of a green scrub suit volunteered to lead him down a flight of steps into a long corridor.

Empty hospital cots lined the sides of the corridor. They stood ready and waiting. At the end of the passageway, Ross followed his guide through a pair of metal swinging doors into a large white-tiled room. Facing him at the far end of the room was a wall of shiny, stainless steel. It took Ross a moment to realize that the shiny, stainless steel surface was divided into drawers with handles. It looked like a huge metal filing cabinet for the dead.

Ross watched silently as a hairy arm reached out and pulled open a drawer in the second row of the filing cabinet. Then the man stepped aside.

Ross stared down at the face of his father lying dumb and deep in his stainless steel cradle. His head was resting on a tiny pillow, the kind the airlines give you on a long trip. His father seemed only asleep, nothing more than that. Had death quite conquered him, such a noisy man? Ross knew that the heart attack had sucked his father's lungs of breath...and yet, the face was still ruddy, still the cheeks of a man stung by the wind and burned by the sun. Ross stooped to kiss the familiar face and felt the naked chill of the grave's foot caught in the corners of his father's mouth. The hard stubble of the unshaven beard scratched against his skin and made his eyes water. Whatever made him think he could kiss a dead man good-bye?

"Please," said Ross as he straightened up and turned toward the male nurse, "close the drawer, I think I have to go now."

He followed his guide as they retraced their steps through the long corridor and up the stairs which led to an exit at street level. Emerging from the building, Ross stared into the blind eye of day.

****

Ross struggled to rouse himself. He leaned forward on the couch, his elbows on his knees, and squeezed his skull between his hands. Then he reached behind him and with a stiff-armed motion pushed himself off the couch. He walked slowly into the foyer and turned on the light. Ross looked at his watch and considered what time it would be in Colorado. Then he picked up the phone and called long distance.

"Hey, Dan, this is your old man. How're things going in Denver?"

"Not bad, how are things with you and Mom?"

"We're all right. Nothing to worry about. Listen, did you watch the game last night?"

Shaving

Standing in front of the stainless steel wall deep in the basement mortuary of the hospital, Ross had no idea what he was looking at. Only when the attendant in the green scrub suit pulled a smooth rolling steel drawer out from inside the wall did Ross fully understand the nature of the wall.

Ross was now able to look upon the still ruddy face of his dead father lying so silently in his temporary coffin of stainless steel. Bending over the open drawer, Ross tried to kiss his father good-bye. As he did so, the hard stubble of his father's beard scratched against his cheek. Almost instantly, his mind was flooded with images of a long forgotten scene.

Ross was a child again, a boy of six or seven. He had climbed up on the wooden toilet seat to watch his father shave. Watching his father shave was one of his favorite things to do. His father stood in front of the bathroom sink wearing nothing but his undershirt and shorts. Ross could see the thick mat of chest hairs curling up and out of the neck of the undershirt.

Now his father reached up to a shelf that was alongside the bathroom mirror and took down a shiny, chrome steel case of no more than two-and-a-half inches by six inches. Ross knew that hidden inside the case was a sharp razor. More than once his father had told him that the beautiful chrome case with the Greek key design impressed on its surface was made in England. He called it a Rolls Razor.

Ross stared fascinated as his father pushed a button at one end of the case which allowed him to remove one of the sides. Removing the side exposed a double pronged handle which was attached to a rolling device attached to the razor's blade. Ross' father began pushing this handle back and forth. As he did so the blade rotated through 180 degrees, slapping its sharp edge against the hard red leather which lined the inside of the case. Slap, slap, slap. Ross loved the sound. His father explained that what he was doing was called 'stropping' and it was effectively sharpening the cutting edge of the razor's blade.

Next, Ross watched as his father detached the sharpened blade from the roller, removed the razor's handle from inside the case, and attached the two pieces to form a complete shaving instrument. The shaving ritual now required the application of soap. To accomplish that Ross' father took down a wooden bowl from the same shelf the Rolls Razor had occupied. The bowl was filled with soap. On its cover was a label that said Yardley.

Opening the medicine cabinet over the sink, his father removed a shaving brush. His father once told him that the brush was made from pure Badger hair and had an ivory handle. Of course, Ross had no idea what a Badger was. However, he suspected it was some kind of animal.

Now came one of the acts of shaving that Ross loved the most. His father turned on the hot water and let it run until it was steaming hot. Then he caught the water in his cupped hands and splashed it all over his face. Holding the badger brush under the faucet, his father soaked it in the hot water and spun it around on the soap inside the wooden bowl. When the soap foamed up, he lathered his face and throat with rapid strokes of the brush. Every so often he stopped, made a face in the mirror and winked at Ross. Then he would reach out and swipe Ross on the cheek with the soap-laden brush.

When his father actually began to shave with the single edged Rolls Razor, Ross grew tense. He worried that his father would cut himself. As the shaving progressed, the area under his father's nose became the razor's target. Ross saw clearly how his father would grab the tip of his nose in one hand, pull it up out of harm's way, draw his upper lip in toward his teeth, and quickly shave with a few downward strokes.

Once, he saw his father cut himself. Little droplets of blood appeared under his nose. His father tore off a tiny piece of toilet paper and briefly held it against the nick. Then he pressed what looked like a white crayon to the spot. He called it a styptic pencil. The bleeding stopped immediately.

After he had finished shaving, his father would rinse his face with cold water, pat it dry with a small towel, and apply an aftershave lotion he called Bay Rum. Then he would lift Ross up in his arms and hold him in front of the medicine cabinet mirror so that he could see himself.

"Someday you will shave just like me," his father said. Kissing Ross on his forehead, his father put him down and said, "Now, go get dressed."

But that was long ago. Ross leaned over the stainless steel drawer and touched his lips to his father's head.

Then he spoke to the attendant in the green scrub suit who had been waiting patiently, "Please close the drawer, I'm through here."

The man dutifully closed the drawer.

Turning his back to the stainless steel wall, Ross left the white-tiled mortuary and walked down the long hallway that led to the stairway which led to the lobby of the hospital. With each step the joy of memory past turned into present pain. Step by step by step by step. When he finally reached the landing at the top of the stairs, Ross raised his hand to brush away the lather that he felt clinging to his face.

Giver of Gifts

He had finally gone and done it, and he knew his wife would not like it. Not one bit.

"You did what?"

"You heard me. I invited her to come live with us."

"But you know what a difficult person she is. She'll make life impossible for us."

"No she won't. She's my mother and I couldn't see what else I could say."

"You couldn't see? Well, I'll tell you what else. You could have said no. Do you have any idea what this will mean? Do you? Have you given any thought at all to where we'll put her or what room we'll give her?"

His wife's antagonism saddened him. At the same time, in a perverse kind of way, it strengthened his resolve.

"Damn it, you don't have to make a federal case out of this. It's not a problem. We'll put her up in one of the boys' bedrooms. Maybe we'll give her David's old room on the top floor."

"Sure we will. And when is all this supposed to happen, that is, if I'm allowed to ask?"

"I told her I'd come pick her up on Sunday. I told her she should pack her things and get ready."

"This Sunday? Isn't that kind of sudden? I mean, have you thought about her furniture and things? What are we going to do with all her stuff?"

"You don't have to worry about it. I'll make all the arrangements when I get to Albany. I'll have her stuff shipped down to us. We can probably store most of it in the basement. That's what basements are for."

"Of course! Why didn't I think of that? You've got this whole thing figured out, haven't you?"

"Now what's that supposed to mean?"

"It means that you haven't got the slightest idea what you're letting us in for. It means things that I can't even begin to tell you, because I know you won't listen. But one thing I can tell you. By trying to be the good son and inviting your grieving mother to come live with us, you, my darling, are making the biggest mistake of your life. Just wait and see if I'm not right. We'll both live to regret it!"

His wife snuffed out her cigarette, turned on her heel, and left him sitting alone in the kitchen. The argument was over.

"Well," he thought, "that wasn't so bad.""At least she hadn't said no. She could have put her foot down and adamantly refused to go along with his plan. He, however, was unable to refuse his mother anything. How could he? He loved her. What other possible reason could there be for asking her to come live with him? He recalled the recent telephone conversation he'd had with his mother:

"Is that you?"

"Yes Mom."

"I think I'm losing my mind"

"What makes you say a thing like that?"

"Because I sit all day alone in the apartment drinking cup after cup of coffee and smoking like a chimney. All the ashtrays are full."

"So empty them. That shouldn't be too difficult."

"No, darling, you just don't understand what I'm trying to say. Nothing seems to be worth the effort anymore. When your father was alive there was a reason to do things. I got dressed; I went out; I did shopping; I cooked his meals; we went to the movies; we visited friends. Now I just sit all day. Oh, Ross, why did he leave me?"

His mother's voice sounded faint and far away, as if the miles of wires between Albany and Brooklyn resisted the current of her distress.

"But Mom, you don't have to sit around. You have friends. Call them up. Invite them over. Or better yet, go visit them. You're not a sick woman. I know how you like to get dressed up and go out looking your best. So go out and have a good time. Enjoy yourself. But for God's sake, try to do something."

"I can't. You still don't understand how I feel. It's no use. Without your father next to me there's no reason for doing those things anymore. Everything is so... empty, so meaningless. I just stare out at the traffic on Western Avenue. I see people with lives to lead coming and going all day long and I think they're telling me something. They're saying my life is over. I have no place left to go."

He almost heard her say, "Your father saw to that," but he had only finished the thought in his own head. What could he say? She seemed to be deliberately trying to break his heart. So he had blurted it out without thought, without consideration of the consequences.

"Look, Mom, why don't you come live with Livia and me? Leave Albany and start a new life for yourself here in Brooklyn. I think that's what Dad would have wanted you to do."

Much to his surprise his mother accepted his offer without a murmur of protest. Without an argument from her, he found himself explaining the arrangements he would have to make in order to pick her up. When he finally got off the phone, he wasn't sure whether the invitation he had made was his own idea or not.

Early in the morning the following Sunday, Ross climbed into his old, beat-up Jeep station wagon and took off for Albany. As he passed the Tappan Zee Bridge his car broke down. The moment he heard the scraping sound accompanied by the roar of the motor he knew that his muffler and tail pipe assembly had separated and hit the pavement. He pulled off the highway, picked up the pieces, and was lucky to find a local garage with a mechanic on duty. He waited impatiently while the rusty parts of the broken exhaust system were jerry-rigged. The mechanic assured him it would hold together long enough to get him to where he was going. Then, it was back to the New York State Thruway and north to Albany again.

As he drove he worried about what he would find waiting for him in his parents' apartment. No point in thinking about the terrible things his wife had said. When his mother crossed the threshold of his house, he would find out soon enough. Instead, his mind dwelled on the suddenness of his father's death and the strange behavior of his mother at the graveside.

****

Dressed in black, her head and shoulders covered by a lace shawl, she stood on that green hillside as still as any granite headstone.

While the rabbi lifted his voice to heaven and implored the Lord of the Universe to grant eternal peace to the soul of the man who lay at his feet, Ross wondered if the God who had created the universe and warm summer days felt himself gently nudged by the ancient Hebrew words. His mother, standing at the foot of the grave, was not comforted by the rabbi's words. Not one bit. Neither her sisters crying into little white handkerchiefs, nor her friends uttering words of sympathy seemed to afford her any consolation. She saw only a gaping hole and a wooden coffin. Just as stiff and silent as that white pine box, she gazed upon it with an unblinking eye.

All that day his mother's demeanor was strange and unaccountable. She appeared completely devoid of personal volition. Wherever people led her, she went. Whatever people told her to do, she did. If someone said, "Ida, sit down," she sat. If someone said, "Ida, eat a little something," she opened her mouth.

****

When Ross arrived at her apartment he wondered whether he would find that the tide of her grief had subsided and the woman he knew as his mother had somehow recovered her normal self. As he rang the doorbell he reminded himself that his father would not be there to greet him with one of his great bear hugs. Ever since he was a little boy Ross had loved to feel those strong arms embrace his shoulders. Now, his bones simply ached.

The door opened and he looked into his mother's face. She had her make-up on too thick. Two blots of rouge stained her cheeks. She had neglected to spread the cosmetic over her face and her unnatural pallor was heightened by the abrupt contrast in color. Ross thought she looked a little the clown. Her dyed red hair served to magnify this effect. She smiled at him rather mechanically, tilted her head up to kiss him, failed to complete the gesture, and turned away to reenter the apartment. As she padded away from him on slippered feet, he noticed a pink, plastic curler still clinging to a lock of hair at the nape of her neck.

She sat down at a white Formica table where she continued drinking her coffee and eating a piece of toast covered with globs of strawberry jam. An ashtray in front of her was piled high with cigarette butts. With an open hand, palm turned upward, she motioned toward the cardboard boxes and bags scattered about the living room.

"As you can see, I'm all packed and ready to go. When I finish my breakfast we'll leave."

Ross looked at his watch. It was almost twelve o'clock, a little late for breakfast. While his mother dawdled over her food, he began to poke around in the cartons she had stuffed with household items. He found the usual assortment of dishes, pots and pans, kitchen utensils, and small electric appliances.

However, two boxes were special. In one, lovingly swaddled in dishtowels, were the porcelain figurines with which his mother loved to clutter the tops of shelves and end tables. In the second box was a highly prized collection of European cut crystal, her favorite kind of possession. Each vase and bowl was carefully wrapped in several layers of white tissue paper. In the hall closet he discovered suitcases and garment bags filled with her clothes. Shoe boxes were piled on top of one another like children's building blocks.

It occurred to Ross that there should be more stuff. Where were his father's things? He crossed over to the den that his father had used as an office. The surface of his desk was covered with the mundane necessities of a salesman's life. A digital clock winked its red L.E.D. eyes at him. A bronze trophy of a man carrying two sample cases surveyed the business paraphernalia spread out around its black, plastic base. There were lined yellow billing pads, a chrome stapler, two ballpoint pens, a white ashtray pockmarked with brown cigarette burns, a black dial phone, some sheets of personal stationery, a box of paper clips, a batch of pencils with broken points held together by a rubber band, and a calendar mounted on a heavy brass base. It was the calendar that drew his attention. It was the kind of device that had flip-flop plastic numbers which could be lifted up and over two parallel brass hoops so that the numbers dropped out of sight on the far side.

The face of the calendar announced that today was June 30, 1971. It was mistaken. That date was one day before the day of his father's death and that was almost two months ago. A brief look around revealed no cartons.

Ross crossed the hall into the bedroom. Light, like some thin liquid seeping through the slats of the Venetian blinds, swathed the room in mist. Shadows puddled in the corners of the darkened room and robbed his vision of its usual ability to discern customary details of shape and texture. Pastel shades of blue washed over the bedspreads, drapes, and walls. Blueness tinted his mother's antique white dresser. Its top was bare, empty of the jewel-like perfume bottles which she used to display on a blue-mirrored tray with a brass filigreed border. It was all gone, packed away in boxes with the other remnants of her life.

Ross turned on the ceiling light and surveyed the rest of the room. His father's dresser stood alone against the far wall. It was a dark mahogany chest-on-chest whose massive bulk dominated the silent room in much the same way his father's presence dominated any room he entered. At least, so it had always seemed to Ross.

Hesitating a moment, he opened the top drawer of the chest and immediately was overcome by the feeling that he was intruding into a private realm that was forbidden territory all the years of his childhood.

Pairs of black socks, stuffed one inside the other and rolled into balls, filled the width of the shallow drawer. The second drawer contained hand-rolled linen handkerchiefs. Pressed and folded they rested on top of one another like soft pages in a diary no one would ever write. The next drawer uncovered a selection of ties arranged according to color. Light blue and dark navy ties were stretched out next to red and maroon ties which were nestled against beige and brown ties.

"My father was a neat man, he kept his tent free from sand."

The line was from a poem Ross had read somewhere and it sprang to mind now. The last of the shallow top drawers contained flat white boxes which Ross felt were vaguely familiar.

He opened each of them slowly, deliberately. Silk ties, intricate jacquards, and regimental stripes were folded inside crisp tissues of white, still new, never worn. These were birthday gifts, Fathers Day gifts, tokens of Ross' undying affection. He picked up a card which was still in one of the boxes. On its cover were the familiar icons of a Golden Retriever, a smoking pipe, and a pair of velvet slippers. Inside the card he had written:

"Dear Dad, Something special from London for the man who has everything. Much love, Ross."

Ross carefully removed the scarf with the English label from its box. It was silk on one side and mohair on the other. He felt its lovely softness and then he crushed it in his hand.

The first of the large lower drawers was filled with white-on-white dress shirts. Laundered and starched they lay stiff in their plastic bags. The second large drawer contained boxes of almost uniform size. Ross guessed their contents even before he opened them. There were madras sport shirts, a terry cloth robe from Turkey, knit cotton Polos by Nautica, an elaborate damask smoking jacket, and all, quite obviously, never worn.

Ross sat down on his father's bed and stared at his gifts. Resting his elbow on his knee and his chin in his hand, he tried to fathom the meaning of it all. He thought that perhaps if he could identify some past experience it might give him a clue to his father's bizarre behavior. All he knew for certain was what he felt, and that was a terrible weight of sadness causing him to sink deeper into himself.

Memories of his own birthdays and gifts his father had given him were as vivid as the illustrated pages of Audubon or National Geographic magazines. He remembered the down payment on the split-level house when he moved to Long Island and got a job teaching out there.

In addition, there was the handsome Spanish oak dining room set with eight leather chairs and a long hunt table .On another occasion his father presented his three grandsons with their own bedroom sets complete with desks. And, of course, how could he forget all the cars. Every time his father bought a new car for himself, he made a deal for a used one for Ross. He could still see his father standing in a car lot surrounded by trade-ins, proudly pointing to his latest find. He could still hear his voice saying,

"This one's yours. She's a beauty, a real cream puff, belonged to some old lady."

The voice inside his head caused his throat to constrict, and Ross began to choke. His body shook as a chill running down his spine severed his contact with the past. He pushed himself up from the bed, saw where he was, and knew what he should be doing. He walked back to the small dinette where his mother was staring out the window at traffic on Western Avenue.

"Mom, I'd rather not pack Dad's things today. I'll do it when I come back up here to ship the furniture. Okay? I'm going to start loading the Jeep right now. Please finish getting dressed so we can leave."

"No, you mustn't put my things in your Jeep. You know how I hate that car of yours. Here, take these."

She pushed a set of car keys toward him across the Formica table.

"They're the keys to your father's new car. It's in the garage out back. Bring it around to the front and put my things in it. Then we'll drive it to New York. You can leave your car here. That's the way your father would want it."

When Ross protested his mother pressed the keys into his hand. He was given no choice. Ross went to the rear of the building and raised the garage door. The door slid up to reveal a shiny, metallic-red Lincoln Continental, Mark III.

"My father's new car," Ross thought, and at the same time, "his last car."

He drove it around to the front of the house and began loading his mother's stuff into it. He could not help noticing that the car possessed every extra feature Detroit had to offer. It had a white leather interior, a tilt steering wheel, cruise control, power windows, and front and rear speakers. The metallic red finish gleamed in the afternoon sun. Here, then, was his Dad's idea of what a successful salesman should drive, a twenty-two foot long American dream machine, a veritable chariot of the gods. And now, all fifty-six hundred pounds of it belonged to him.

His mother had said, "Your father wanted you to have it. Those were his last words: *Give Ross the Lincoln.*"

Although Ross didn't believe that these were anything close to his father's last words, he knew them to be true to his father's steadfast generosity.

By mid afternoon they were on their way. The apartment was locked, his mother's boxes and bags stowed on board, and the car accelerating onto the New York State Thruway.

Ross set the cruise control at 65 and figured that they would hit Brooklyn in about four and a half hours. Maybe five.

He was impressed by the way the Lincoln performed. Quietly, effortlessly, the big V8 sucked up the miles. Only the drone of the tires in steady communion with the asphalt reminded him that they were speeding through space. The roadside trappings of the highway seemed to rush up to meet the hurtling vehicle. Trees, telephone poles, power lines, and industrial parks slipped silently through the windshield and disappeared in the rearview mirror, their reality made transitory by distance, time, and acceleration.

Ross dreamed he was strapped into a modern time machine which was without motion of its own. The earth alone spun to meet him, revealing the assorted accouterments of this world through each degree of turning. It presented a panorama of converging lines and diminishing perspectives where earth and sky met on a horizon line just two inches above the nose of the Lincoln's hood. He vaguely sensed that his perception was being warped by a dimensional scheme in which solid objects were illusory and their relationships deceptive. He broke out into a sweat and clutched the steering wheel tightly trying to hold onto reality with both hands. He looked at his mother sitting silently next to him. Although they hadn't spoken much, she, at least, was real.

Ross wondered how she would manage once he got her home. He knew she felt abandoned by his father, left to navigate an emotional landscape of conflicting recollections and uncertain new directions. In such a world would the son really be able to assuage her grief and allay her fears?

Hours passed. His mother remained lost in reverie. Sooner than he had anticipated, Ross was pulling into his own driveway. He immediately began unloading the car. His wife came out of the house to greet them, extending herself to make his mother feel comfortable and at home. Things went smoothly.

The next day Ross placed an ad in BUY LINES, a New York newspaper which specialized in selling automobiles:

Lincoln 71, Continental Mark III, Brand new, Leather int, ps/pb/ac Stereo, Tilt, Cruise. MUST SELL, Death in family. Call eves.284-8206

Two days later, the big car was sold. Ross stepped out into the street and watched his father's chariot disappear as its new owner turned the corner. Ross waved good-bye. He waved good-bye to the Lincoln and he waved good-bye to his father, the giver of gifts.

Thirteen

I don't think I ever saw my father look at a map. Wherever he was going he always seemed to know how to get there. When we left Chicago on our way to New York he never stopped to ask for directions. He just kept on driving, driving through the night. That's the part of the trip I remember best. The moon that night was a big silver dish casting its silvery beams over the landscape and the highway was a river of moonlight leading to grandma's house in Brooklyn, almost 800 miles away.

All our belongings were packed in luggage in the trunk of the Buick. I was ten at the time and my five year old sister was sleeping with her head in my lap. Watching the moon from my seat in the back of the car, I imagined it was playing hide- and-go- seek with me as it continually managed to slip in and out of the tops of the trees that bordered the road. While my father kept driving eastward, the moon continued riding the southern sky on my side of the car. Through Indiana, Ohio, Pennsylvania, and New Jersey the moon helped light the way. I don't remember my father pulling off the road for gas, or for food, or for a place to sleep. All I remember of that nighttime trip was the moon following along like a faithful dog.

As my father drove through the night, he would sometimes break the silence inside the car by saying, "Idee." He never called my mother Ida. My mother understood her name to be a signal for her to light up a cigarette and pass it to him. When he inhaled a few deep drags, I could see the tip of the cigarette burn brighter, its red glow reflected in the windshield of the car. I soon came to realize that my dad would ask my mother for a cigarette approximately every fifty miles. I knew this to be true because the Buick had an odometer whose numbers were set into the face of a big speedometer which I could easily read by looking through the space separating the shoulders of my parents. It wasn't too hard for me to do some arithmetic inside my head and figure out that if my father continued driving at the rate he was driving and smoking cigarettes at the rate he was smoking them, then in the time it took for him to smoke fifteen or sixteen cigarettes we would be in New York.

As my father drove through the night and my mother remained silent and my sister continued sleeping, I thought about the reasons I had been given for why we were leaving Chicago.

"Your father has lost his business," my mother said. "You must know that your father owned his own brokerage firm and the S.E.C. went ahead and changed the rules about how people could buy stocks and bonds on margin."

There was anger in her voice. The year was 1936. I was ten years old and didn't understand a word of what my mother was telling me. She went on to say that my father's business partner had run away with all the money clients had entrusted to my father. This man had disappeared and so had all the money. Now, stealing was something I could understand. And that, my mother said, was why we were on our way to grandma's house.

****

A few months after we moved into the home of my grandmother, my father mysteriously disappeared without taking his clothes out of the closet and without saying good-bye. When I asked my mother what had happened to my father and where he had gone, she replied that he was on the road. He had gone to Tennessee to buy Jack Daniel's warehouse receipts.

"What are warehouse receipts and who is Jack Daniels," I asked.

My mother explained that Jack Daniels was a friend of my father and warehouse receipts were pieces of paper that showed how many barrels of whiskey were owned by the bearer of the receipt. For a while her answer satisfied me. However, when more time passed by and my father still had not come home, I asked her the same questions again. This time she said more or less the same thing, but with some variations in the particulars.

"Your father is on the road. He has gone to Kentucky to buy some Jim Beam warehouse receipts for barrels of Kentucky bourbon."

"Is Jim Beam also a friend of dad's?" I asked.

"Yes."

Time went on. I was beginning to get used to the idea of life without my dad around. When my thirteenth birthday arrived my mother told me that she was going to take me to Radio City Music Hall in Manhattan to celebrate my birthday. At night she helped me lay out my only suit, best shirt, and tie to match. In the morning she went off to work and told me to meet her at the store at twelve o'clock.

"Don't be late!"

Ever since my dad had gone away, my mother worked selling expensive coordinating bags for high priced shoes at Jack Schaefer's, a classy store on Fifth Avenue and 47th Street.

When I got to the store a little early the next morning, my mother told me to wait for her in a malted milk shop around the corner. Then she handed me a package all dressed up in fancy wrapping paper.

"A present," she said.

While walking to the shop around the corner I started removing the paper from the package and discovered a tablet of fine, smooth sheets of drawing paper about 12 by 15 inches in size. Attached to the Bristol board cover with Scotch tape were a 4B and 6B pencil and a kneaded eraser. When the malted milk shake I had ordered was placed on the counter before me, I stared in awe at its triple-tier design of a large glass ball placed on top of a medium sized glass ball on top of a small glass ball terminating in a flat round base. Never having seen such a configuration before and finding it interesting, I immediately began to draw it, making sure that the ellipse that described the opening at the top of the glass was not pointed at its outer ends. After a short while, when my sketch was almost complete, I looked up from my drawing to see a strange thing happening in front of the shop's large plate glass window.

Out on the sidewalk a well-dressed man was removing his suit jacket and rolling it up. Taking off his fedora and holding it tight to his chest, he calmly lay down on the sidewalk while placing his folded suit under his head to serve as a pillow. No sooner did he prostrate himself than he underwent a series of convulsions. A small crowd quickly gathered around him. I ran outside to get a better view of what was going on. One man announced to everyone and to no one in particular that he was an E.M.T. and, thereby, qualified to handle the situation. To my amazement, he knelt down and grabbed hold of the tongue of the man with a handkerchief from his own pocket.

A few more moments elapsed and the spasmodic contractions ceased. The well-dressed man got to his feet, helped by the E.M.T. He put his hat back on his head, unfolded his jacket and put his arms through the sleeves. Then he dusted off the lapels of his jacket, thanked the young man who had helped him, and blithely walked away as if nothing of any consequence had occurred. The people who had been watching quickly dispersed.

When I returned to the shoe store and described to my mother what I had witnessed, she told me that what I had just seen was a man experiencing an epileptic episode. She added that it was not unusual for such a person to feel a premonition moments before the actual event occurred.

Then she said, "Let's go eat lunch."

Leaving 47th street and Fifth Avenue we headed toward 50th and Sixth where Radio City Music Hall was located. On the way she pulled me into a small restaurant where we were greeted by a hostess who seemed to know my mother. As we were being seated I noticed a man wearing a paisley jacket covered in glittering blue and green sequins. He wore a great white turban on his head with a big oval shaped mirror stuck in its center and he was going from table to table, bending over and talking to people. My mother politely motioned for him to come and visit our table.

As he approached us my mother said, "Please sit down and tell my son's fortune."

I should say that when we first sat down I had placed my sketch of the soda fountain's malted milk container face up on the table. As the fortune teller started to seat himself I pushed the drawing tablet to one side, in front of the empty fourth chair. Then the man in the big turban and glittering jacket took my hand in his and turned it up in order to read what fortune had written in the palm of my hand.

"Hmm, let me see. Ah, this line tells me you are talented. Someday you will become a famous artist!"

Of course, I had seen him glance at my drawing as he was sitting down.

When we had finished our lunch and were leaving the restaurant, my mother asked me what I thought about the fortune teller. I told her that I thought he was a fake. My mother laughed and said that men such as he were often called fakers by other men. Then, as we continued to walk toward Radio City Music Hall and 50th Street, my mother began to tell me about the fabulous Rockettes. She said they were best known for their synchronized precision dancing. Once again, I could not picture what my mother was trying to describe. Unfortunately, I don't remember what movie we saw that day. Something with Gregory Peck, I think. However, I do remember being impressed by the cavernous reaches of that famous theater. All in all, it was a great day. On the West End subway ride home to Brooklyn my mother fell asleep.

****

My thirteenth birthday was over. In September of '39, I began attending Boys High School in Brooklyn. Coming home from school one day a few months into the new term, I saw a man sitting on the wooden bench in front of the stoop that led up to grandma's house. He was smoking a cigarette and blowing smoke rings. I was surprised to suddenly recognize him as my long traveling father. Home from the road. Home from buying all those barrels of whiskey. Or so I thought. Happy and excited, I ran to meet him. When he saw me coming, he stood up and held me by my shoulders.

"Look at you. Look at how you've grown...you're so tall."

I remember how he wrapped those strong arms of his around me and crushed me to his chest. Then, still holding on to me, he kissed me on top of my head. I could smell the nearness of him, the acrid odor of cigarette smoke that he wore like an old sweater. He was my father and (as I write this down) I feel like I'm thirteen again...if only for a brief moment.

Nightmare

Little Jackie got a Daisy Air Rifle complete with BB rolls for his tenth birthday. It made him very happy. Tucking the rifle under his arm and filling his pockets with the BB's, he ran out of the apartment house where he lived to the empty lot across the street. The lot was nothing more than an empty space between the tall walls of two apartment buildings. How the lot came to be, no one knew. Little Jackie certainly didn't care. He knew every stone, every piece of broken glass in the place. The lot helped him dream away the long days of summer.

Jackie stood a milk bottle on a rock at one end of the lot. Very carefully he counted off twenty paces as he had once seen a soldier do in a movie. Then he lay down on his stomach and cradled the butt of the rifle in his right shoulder while his left hand supported the metal barrel. He lined the front sight up with the rear sight and pressed it against his cheek. Squinting with one eye, he steadied the rifle, held his breath, and slowly squeezed the trigger. There was a hollow pop from the air rifle and a loud ping off the bottle. Little Jackie was a natural born marksman. He spent the entire afternoon completely absorbed in riddling milk bottles with BB pellets.

In a corner of the lot grew one little scraggly tree. It even had a forlorn scattering of green leaves. A small sparrow took refuge from the heat of the afternoon sun in the shade of its leaves. Little Jackie looked up and saw the sparrow perched on a thin branch.

Quietly, ever so stealthily, he crawled toward the tree. When he calculated that the bird was within shooting range, he flattened himself against the ground and took careful aim. With the pop of the rifle the little bird came fluttering down. Jackie stood up and went to the fallen sparrow. He bent over and prodded its belly with his finger. He was amazed to see how white its feathers were on its underside. A tiny red spot glistened in the center of all the whiteness. In a vague way Jackie felt there was something else he should do. Then, he knew what.

Little Jackie searched up and down in the alley in back of the lot. He rummaged through garbage pails and piles of litter until he found what he was looking for. It was a wooden cheese box, the kind that closed with a sliding top. Jackie returned to the lot and picked up the dead sparrow. Holding it by the tip of one wing, he plunked it into the box and slid the cover shut. Then he dug a hole under the tree with a shard of broken glass. He placed the box in the hole and covered it with dirt, patting it down and smoothing it out with his hands. Little Jackie stood up and surveyed the sparrow's grave. He still was not satisfied with his work. Something was missing.

Returning to the alley, he found a broken egg crate and tore off two little pieces of wood. From inside his pants pocket he withdrew a large rubber band which he sometimes used to shoot paper clips at his classmates. With the help of the rubber band he cleverly attached the two sticks to each other in the shape of a cross. Then he planted the cross over the grave of the little brown bird. Little Jackie was very pleased. He crooned a half-forgotten nursery rhyme to himself:

> "I shot an arrow in the air,
> It fell to earth,
> I know not where."

Little Jackie was wearing his new fielder's glove which he had just been given for his twelfth birthday. He was in the lot with his friend and they were playing catch with a baseball. His friend made a wild throw and the ball crashed through a pane of glass in a window somewhere. The two boys stopped their game and sat down on a broken orange crate in a corner of the lot.

Across the street from the lot a milkman and his horse and wagon were making deliveries. Jackie could hear the clinking of bottles in metal baskets every time the milkman pulled one out of the wagon. Jackie saw that the horse had a very ugly head and a big red eye and the eye was watching him. In fact, it was staring at him. The eye made Little Jackie angry. He picked up a stone and threw it at the horse. It struck the horse right in its bloodshot eye!

Instantly, Jackie knew he had made a terrible mistake. The big brown milkman's horse glared at him. Jackie clearly saw that the horse knew that he was the one who had thrown the stone. Without any hesitation at all, the big horse swung its wagon around and started across the street toward him with powerful strides. Its great head and neck were thrust forward and giant muscles bulged across its broad chest. Little Jackie was woefully scared. He began to retreat across the empty lot. As the huge horse chased after him, Jackie began to run.

He ran down the alley in back of the lot. The horse, pulling the wagon behind him, galloped after Jackie, its hooves making loud clopping sounds on the alley's cobblestones. Jackie was running as fast as he could, gasping for breath, yet the giant horse was gaining on him. He was afraid to look back. The alley stretched out before him, its sides lined with buildings, and Jackie thought there was no escape.

Then, unexpectedly and all at once, Little Jackie saw safety in a dark passageway whose entrance was three steps down from the alley in the side of an apartment house. It was the kind of narrow opening in a building's wall that custodians use for removing large cans of ashes and cinders collected from a buildings furnace.

"It can't get me in there," Jackie thought, "the wagon will stop it and won't let it get in."

Little Jackie ducked down the steps into the dark interior of the narrow space. There was no exit, only a blind wall of cement opposite the light from the entranceway. He tried the handle of a metal door that led to what must be the building's basement. He pulled on it with all his might, but it wouldn't budge. As he strained against the door there was a horrible crashing sound of splintering wood and the entrance to the passageway was filled by the form of the milkman's giant horse. It plunged and thrashed at him, snorting and spewing great globs of spittle from its slavering mouth while its wild eyes rolled in their sockets. Jackie dropped to the floor and huddled against the blind wall to avoid the flailing hooves of the angry beast. Inches away from his head the flashing steel horseshoes struck hot sparks from the cement walls of the enclosure.

Little Jackie opened his mouth to scream, but no sound came out, only a silent puff of white feathers fluttered up.

Einstein, Uncertainty, & Ross

In July of 1943 Ross Seymour enlisted in the United States Army. He had just completed his first semester at the Guggenheim School of Aeronautics and he was anxious to get out of school and join his friends, who had all enlisted in the army and were now fighting in Europe. At the induction center in Fort Dix, New Jersey, Ross was given a battery of written tests, and before one could say 'Jackie Robinson' he was shipped off to Princeton, New Jersey, where he suddenly found himself a cadet in the Army Specialized Training Reserve Program at the University of Princeton. The stated intention of the program was to turn 250 cadets into mechanical engineers.

Ross soon fell into a daily routine which included jogging from Foulke Hall, a dormitory building, to the Princeton polo grounds less than a mile away. Need I say that during World War II the stables were empty? It was on one of his early morning runs before classes began that Ross first encountered Albert Einstein. It seemed to be generally acknowledged around campus that Einstein was doing research at the Princeton School of Advanced Studies.

Have I said that it was the middle of December and it was as cold on campus as on any Russian tundra? Snow was everywhere. Piled up on the sides of the quadrangle, it was frozen into a white, cement-like border. Einstein was dressed for the weather. He wore a navy Pea coat, a scarf, a woolen watchman's hat pulled down over his ears, and boots up to his knees. Ross noticed that wisps of hair escaping from the man's hat were blowing in the wind. While Einstein certainly wasn't jogging, he did walk rapidly, taking long strides with each step.

As Ross approached Einstein, he said, "Good morning professor." And then, hoping to engage Einstein in conversation, he added, "Cold out, isn't it?"

"Ja," said the great man as he continued on his way without slowing down a step. Thus ended Ross' first conversation with Albert Einstein.

His second encounter with Einstein occurred under much the same circumstances. Again it was a cold winter's morning and the famous professor was out taking his morning constitutional walk. As fate would have it, Ross was also out jogging that morning and slowed his pace in order to fall into step alongside Einstein.

Einstein took a quick sidewise glance at Ross and said with a certain amount of disciplined restraint in his voice, "Young man, why are you following me?"

Ross replied that he was not following him and that their meeting was purely by chance, completely accidental. However, Ross immediately added, "I would very much like to speak with you so that I might ask you to explain a problem I am having with a particular scientific theory."

Einstein, his curiosity piqued by such a question, hesitated for a second and then motioned to a wrought iron and wood bench that stood at the edge of the path. Both men sat down.

What follows is not a verbatim recital of what was said on that day so long ago. It is, rather, a determined attempt to present the central ideas of that conversation with Einstein, as Ross recalled their significance through the kaleidoscope of his Princeton memories. At this point perhaps I should mention that Ross and I were old friends. Both of us had graduated from Boys High in Brooklyn and had arrived at Princeton at the same time. It was during our senior year at Boys that Ross had patiently explained to me the concepts that were so fundamental to understanding the niceties of differential calculus.

"And what is this theory that seems to be troubling you," Einstein asked.

Ross replied that he was studying physics at the engineering school and was having difficulty understanding quantum mechanics. In addition, the uncertainty principle that seemed to be an intrinsic part of the theory served only to baffle him. A slow smile spread from the corners of Einstein's mouth.

"Nobody truly understands quantum," he said. "It attempts to explain the spooky behavior of matter and energy at the subatomic level through a mathematical description of the wave-particle duality and the uncertainty principle of Heisenberg. Moreover, I personally have doubts about the validity of its most fundamental premise. Perhaps you have heard me say that God does not play dice with the universe?"

"Yes, professor, I think everybody knows how you feel about that."

"Is there anything else I can help you with?" Einstein asked.

"Yes, there is," Ross replied. He did not want to lose this incredible opportunity to question Einstein about the physical world. "I would like to learn what your opinion is about some of the ideas I have relative to the space-time continuum and the intrinsic nature of the universe."

"Ah, the nature of the universe," repeated Einstein. "Coincidentally, I am working on that little mystery myself. However, I believe that at this early hour of the morning I can spare a few moments to listen to what you have to say."

And so, with Einstein's gracious indulgence Ross launched into his unusual ideas about space, matter, and time.

"Professor, please excuse my ignorance about the laws of physics, but I am not a trained scientist and so my thinking on the enigma of the universe is based on what is primarily a philosophical approach, rather than a purely mathematical one. I know, for example, that physicists are absolutely determined to find an answer to the ultimate question of how the universe originated. But I seriously believe that this pursuit is a chimera that can only end in deep disappointment. As far as I can determine from all my readings on the subject, the origin of the universe has proven to be a bottomless pit whose mysteries only become deeper the more they are studied."

Ross audaciously continued as Einstein appeared to be listening. "And added to this difficulty is the pervasive influence of the Western narrative that has seriously penetrated every modern person's subconscious. By this I mean that from the time of Homer's 'Iliad' to the time of, say Melville's 'Moby Dick,' even to the very present, every story teller's story is conceived of as having a beginning, a middle, and an end. I question why this must be so. Is it not more sensible to assume that there may be a logic underlying the complex laws of the universe which cannot be written down in some abbreviated paradigm by human beings, and which may, indeed, defy inclusion in any rational theory?"

Einstein, who had been staring intently at Ross during his little recitation, said, "So...?"

"So I think," and here Ross lowered his voice and almost began to whisper, so afraid was he that Einstein would take his ideas for nothing more than the immature ravings of an arrogant freshman, "there never was a beginning to the universe! There was no spectacular phenomenon which scientists like to describe as some kind of huge cataclysmic event that accounts for the origin of the universe. In fact, I find it much more reasonable to assume that space has always been out there, like an ageless and infinitely boundless sea. And since space can have no real meaning for existence without something like a universe to occupy it, incredibly large quantities of matter must always have inhabited space, no doubt in the form of all the different elementary particles that science has already discovered. In this universe of inextricably involved cosmic relationships, it seems to me, matter becomes its own 'raison d'etre'."

"And what does that seem to imply...?" queried Einstein.

If I remember correctly, at this point Ross said that he hesitated, uncertain of his own swirling thoughts. What he was about to describe was a conception of time as a kind of concentrated essence which defied commonly held beliefs. He wanted to get across to Einstein his uniquely original ideas about time's intimate connection with space and matter. He was desperate to have Einstein hear him out before the short time which he had been granted expired. He tried hard to assemble his personal thoughts into some semblance of a logical sequence.

"You know, professor, I am studying mechanical engineering at Princeton and one thing I have learned, without the slightest doubt of contradiction, is that engineers tend to think of time as elapsed time. Only elapsed time seems to matter to them. How long does it take for a given object moving at a given rate to get from point A to point B? What is the distance covered in that elapsed time? It would appear that time, distance, and rate are very important aspects of events that describe life here on Earth. So I started to think about these things on a much grander scale in terms of what is known about our universe. And slowly I began to understand that both distance and time are nothing more than inherent functions of matter. Without matter to move through a distance provided by space, and without a moment in time for that motion to occur, it became apparent to me that at the heart of all things lay those elemental particles we call matter. Without the presence of matter, space and time dissolve, and reality ceases to exist."

At this juncture, according to Ross, Einstein took a Meerschaum pipe out of his coat pocket, stuffed some tobacco from a leather pouch into it, lit a wooden match on the side of a small match box, and put the flame to the bowl of his pipe. While he took a few puffs, Ross waited for Einstein's attention to return to him. Finally, pointing the stem of his pipe at Ross, Einstein asked Ross to be a little more explicit about the function of time in his scheme of a world without origin.

Again, according to Ross, Einstein was looking at him with a disquieting, stony stare. For the first time since they sat down on the bench together, Ross felt that this wonderful man was becoming impatient with him. Ross hurried to address what so far he had failed to express.

"It is simply this. I feel that people are deceived by the role of time. They think of time as something that begins in the past, becomes the present, and promises to transform the future. In this familiar scenario of human experience, our day to day reality is bound by time's three incarnations, that is, past, present and future. I believe this to be a seriously flawed interpretation of what is really happening, like some magician's trick of misdirection that is contrived to mislead the audience."

"So what would you have people believe instead?" Einstein asked.

"Simply put, I believe the only time that is real time is present time. You and I both live in the present and so must the universe. A minute from now or a second from now we will still be living in the present. It is impossible for it to be otherwise. No one and no thing has successfully managed to bridge time and live in some future moment. The next second unceremoniously slips into the current second, the present one in which you and I exist. The next second once more becomes the present one. It is a continuous and never ending process. One that can never be interrupted. Imagination itself rebels at the thought. Time, in effect, is always present time. And the same reasoning must necessarily apply to cosmic time. If there were an all-seeing-eye situated somewhere out there in the infinite ocean of space, would it not see all matter and all events across the broad spectrum of the Universe happening in a moment of present time? Without the presence of this present moment in time, I think the world would disappear." There, he had said it.

Professor Albert Einstein got up from the park bench. He knocked the ashes from his pipe against his open palm. He dusted a few ashes away from his Pea coat. Then he put one hand on Ross' shoulder and said, "Young man, you are neither a mathematician nor a physicist and I am afraid you have made it my responsibility to inform you that your ideas about a universe without an origin are misguided. Moreover, I must add that your ideas about time are most strange and fly in the face of conventional thought."

With that said the world famous Einstein took leave of Ross. As he walked away he suddenly stopped and partially turned in order to throw a last remark over his shoulder.

"On the other hand," he said, "I am inclined to admit that there is a remote possibility you might be right about a thing or two."

Ross said that he stood there frozen in his G.I. boots. It wasn't December's icy winds that chilled him to the bone. It was Einstein's final words. As he hurried back to Foulke Hall in order to make roll call, he could not get Einstein's words out of his mind. "You might be right.. you might be right... you might be..." Who in the world was going to believe him?

Ruthie's Pair

> *Thy two breasts are like*
> *two young roes that are twins*
> *which feed among the lilies.*
> *Until the day breaks*
> *and the shadows flee away*
> *I will get me to the mountain of myrrh*
> *and to the hill of frankincense..*
> (Song of Solomon 4:5, 6 KJV)

Ruthie had magnificent breasts. All the guys agreed that in all of Christendom, Judea, and Brooklyn, there flourished not such another pair. On our map of the known world, north was Manhattan; south was Coney Island, and east and west were Ruthie's breasts, two cardinal points that always guided us home to Borough Park.

I remember one summer in June when all of us were sprawled on the stone stoop in front of Jake's house. It was just after graduation from high school; we were seventeen or eighteen years old and our conversation dwelled upon serious academic matters.

"Have any of you guys ever traveled out west?" Jake inquired.

"Nope," we all responded, feeling a little ashamed of our parochial lives.

"Well, if any of you jokers had ever left Brooklyn and traveled around the country like me, you'd know that Ruthie's breasts are the Grand Tetons of breastdom. In fact, lesser chains just can't compare to them."

"What's a lesser chain," prompted Zahn, playing straight man to Jake's learned geologist.

"Lesser chains, you poor slob, can be found right here on our block. Consider Rita, a fair maid whose bosom swells above a slender waist. Her breasts are nice and round, right?"

"Right," we echoed, still not sure what Jake was driving at.

"Now take Gloria," Jake continued, about to offer us another example in support of his thesis. "I've been trying to take Gloria for years," Zahn interrupted. He wiggled his eyebrows up and down and shook some ash from an imaginary cigar.

Jake wasn't amused by Zahn's brief impersonation of Groucho. "Please don't interrupt with your inane remarks when I'm trying to make a point. As I was saying, Gloria's breasts are veritable mountains of myrrh, big and firm, right?"

"Myrrh," we all repeated. "What the hell is myrrh?"

Jake looked at us in disgust. He was about to say more when Sandy stood up, climbed to a step that brought his face level with Jake's and said, "Okay, wise guy, get to the point. We're not stupid y'know. What have Rita and Gloria got to do with Ruthie?"

A gleam came into Jake's eyes as he surveyed our intelligent, if somewhat perplexed, faces.

"It's simple. Rita's breasts and Gloria's breasts are lesser chains because they do not possess the combined physical attributes of Ruthie's classic pair. Ruthie's are so round, so firm, so fully packed, they should be pictured on every Lucky Strike billboard in New York City."

Jake had suddenly switched from resident geologist to advertising guru. We nodded our heads in tacit agreement as we listened to the fanciful twist he had given to the popular cigarette slogan. We recognized the essential truth of his hyperbole. It was, after all, little more than an aesthetic opinion about a physical reality.

Our minds filled with the vision of Ruthie's pair staring out from giant posters. Whether one imagined two perfect spheres suspended by twin golden chains from her shoulders or two swelling globes ensconced in a silk chemise, it was enough to boggle the mind of any seventeen year old man-child.

"Yeah, they sure are something."

We looked down at the bottom step of the stoop to see from whence this intrusion into our philosophical deliberations had come. The thin, high pitched voice belonged to Freddie, Zahn's kid brother. He had been idly playing with his Duncan yo-yo.

"Listen, twerp, what could you possibly know about Ruthie's breasts or anybody's breasts for that matter?"

How dare this juvenile, a mere kid brother, comment upon our mature observations?

"Aw, nothing, nothing at all. I was just thinking, that's all," said little Freddie.

We all smiled indulgently at him. We knew what the kid had been thinking, having thought the same thoughts over a thousand nights while tossing and turning in bed. Now Bernie piped in with his two cents worth. Bernie was a guy who prided himself on his understanding of human psychology as well as just about everything else on planet earth. He was not about to let Freddie's innocent remark slide by without some kind of critical comment.

"Nothing at all, eh? Listen, kiddo, nothing means something. Everything means something. Do you know what evolution means?"

"No," Freddie answered.

"Haven't they taught you about evolution in school?"

"No," Freddie said feebly.

"Well, have you ever heard the name Charles Darwin?"

"No."

Poor Freddie. He was afraid the big boys were about to embarrass him again in some subtly malevolent way. All at once, and completely unasked for, Bernie launched into an explication of Darwin's theory of evolution, ostensibly for the edification of young and naive Freddie. Now Bernie had been a member of Arista all four years at Boys High and we knew him to be no dummy. We also knew him well enough to know he had some abstruse, but nevertheless, pertinent correlation in mind between Ruthie's pair and Darwin's theory when he decided to give his account of evolution.

"Well, according to Darwin, different animals are supposed to have survived on earth because they were the strongest of their kind. After millions of years they developed special characteristics or traits which enabled them to cope with any hardships they might encounter in their daily lives. Y'understand what I'm trying to say to you?"

Bernie paused to give Freddie time to consider and possibly comprehend the incomprehensible. Maybe he expected a response. When it was clearly obvious from the tortured expression on Freddie's face that none would be forthcoming, Bernie remained undaunted. He continued lecturing in his highly pedantic way despite what he must have perceived as a hopelessly lost cause.

"Only those animals survived which fit into their own ecological niche. Darwin called this the survival of the fittest. Y' get it? This is not just a theory. It's a matter of scientific fact...and Ruthie's pair proves it."

At the mention of Ruthie's name, our ears perked up, a vestigial evolutionary trait, no doubt.

"Ruthie's breasts are not just some accidental phenomenon of an errant nature. They are a classic illustration of the evolutionary process. It must have taken mankind millions of years of natural selection to develop a pair such as hers."

Bernie stopped. He grinned. His hands were resting on his chest, fingers extended upward, cup-like, as if he were holding a grapefruit in each hand. We stared at him in open-mouthed admiration. He had made the connection we couldn't see coming. What a brain!

Night time on our block was a time for serious action, when the guys turned into Don Juans, Lotharios, and other lovers of dangerous escapades. Around 11:30 P.M., when the streets of Borough Park were empty of bearded men in black coats and beaver hats, Jake and Sandy and Bernie and Zahn would meet in my back yard. Keeping to the shadows of three-story frame houses, we would silently cross Zahn's back yard and then Bernie's back yard and stealthily traverse the cement driveway which ran along the side of Ruthie's house. Her bedroom window was at the rear of the house and was shielded from any ambient street light by a cluster of small Rose-of-Sharon trees which grew close to the stucco wall next to her window. The lower sill of that window was approximately fifteen inches above our heads. Fate, it seemed, had conspired to arrange circumstances to suit our nefarious purpose.

Directly under Ruthie's window we placed a rusty, but nevertheless, trusty milk box, a sturdy contraption of wood and metal which we kept carefully hidden in Bernie's yard under a clump of Ilex bushes. Now, the moment of truth was at hand. Ruthie's shade was drawn. As always, it was down to a half inch from touching the bottom sill. Lest you have any thoughts to the contrary, I must immediately state that Ruthie was a good girl and quite ignorant of the position she had achieved in our minds with regard to the evolutionary scheme of things. I am also convinced that when she undressed at night she was oblivious of the ungodly lust she inspired in the loins of callow fellows such as us.

Taking turns at standing on the milk box, each of us was able to peer through that half inch of open shade into Ruthie's bedroom. And what a sight was there! Standing in front of the dresser mirror, her back to the window, her reflection facing us, her eyes intent on the image in the glass, she would reach behind her back and unhook her bra. Placing the bra on the dresser she would begin caressing herself. Ever so slowly she would pass her hands back and forth over that magnificent pair, gently fondling them. Watching her, my legs would tremble and my knees grow weak. Finally, mercifully, Ruthie would turn off the lights and go to bed. Only then did our voyeurism end.

And while Ruthie dreamed, the guys outside her window would fall to their knees onto the cement driveway and praise heaven for bestowing upon us that half an inch of open shade through which to gaze in rapture at those fawnlike twins.

Like some long-time-running picture show or a Saturday serial at the local movie theater, there were many such nights spent staring in wonder at Ruthie's pair. But one night I will never forget, presented an opportunity to do more than stare in silent admiration.

Ah, well I remember, it was in bleak December and Ruthie had the chicken pox. I knew because Jake told me so. Moved by some vague humanitarian impulse, I hurried down the block to Ruthie's house, hoping to cheer her up. I rang the doorbell and her mother answered it.

"Hi, Mrs. Snyder, I heard that Ruthie's sick and I've come to cheer her up."

Mrs. Snyder's body blocked the doorway. She was twice as wide as I was.

"You can't see my Ruthie. Ruthie has the chicken pox and it's very, very contagious. No one is allowed to see her."

Somehow I managed to think of a brilliant gambit to counter her negative attitude.

"Oh, it's all right. I've had the chicken pox and now I'm immune to it. There's no reason to be concerned. You don't have to worry about me."

Mrs. Snyder's brow furrowed up in an expression of doubt. What I perceived as a momentary advantage I quickly pursued with an inspired stratagem.

"It was Dr. Kresge who treated me and he said it was impossible to get chicken pox twice."

I knew that Dr. Kresge enjoyed a reputation as a 'big' man, a veritable prima inter pares among physicians in our neighborhood. The legendary name worked like magic. Mrs. Snyder stepped back from the doorway and motioned for me to come inside.

"But you can only stay for a little while. My Ruthie has to get her rest."

"Don't worry, Mrs. Snyder. I won't be long."

I brushed past her and headed for Ruthie's bedroom. Needless to say, I knew where it was. Ruthie was sitting up in bed, some pillows propped behind her back, reading a book. She looked up and smiled at me when I entered. She patted the bed next to her legs, motioning for me to sit down.

"Watcha doing?" I asked.

"Reading a book."

I immediately noticed that she was wearing a bed jacket over a transparently thin blouse which fell from the nipples of her breasts to her lap without ever touching her sides. The second thing I noticed was a dark brown scab nestled in the cleavage between her breasts like some lonely shepherd lost in a valley between gently sloping hills.

"What are you staring at," she asked.

"That scab," I said, pointing to it.

"Isn't it terrible," Ruthie complained.

"No, no, it will be all right, you'll see."

Wishing to comfort her, I took one of her hands in mine.

"A lot you know. You're not a doctor. It will never go away."

Poor Ruthie. She seemed so miserable. I began to stroke her blonde hair with my free hand.

"The doctor says I have to leave the scabs alone, but they itch something awful."

I felt I should do something to alleviate her suffering.

"Listen, let me kiss the boo-boo and make it better."

Before Ruthie had a chance to object, I leaned over her chest and kissed the offending scab. Then I gently brushed against one breast with my lips. Then the other. I kissed the scab again. When there was no protest from above my head, I licked the soft slope on the left. Then I licked and kissed my way up the slope on the right. Pretty soon the slopes began to rise and fall with my kissing and licking. The hills were alive with Ruthie's rapid breathing. As I felt her passion growing, I grew a little passionate myself. I guess I started to slobber or something. Anyway, Ruthie suddenly screamed.

"You stupid bastard, look what you've done!"

"What? What is it?" I was hopelessly preoccupied.

"You've licked off the scab between my breasts. Now I'll be scarred for life!"

Ruthie's words stabbed into my soul, rousing me from my brief sojourn between the hills where I had been savoring the lilies. I raised my head and stared down at what my ignominious actions had wrought. A pink depression the size and shape of half a peanut stared blindly back at me. What had I done? Ruthie's scab, that shy shepherd of healing, slathered away in a moment of simple pleasure, was quite gone. Surely my name would live in infamy. When I walked down any street in Borough Park, people would point to me and say, "There goes the man who licked away Ruthie's scab. The pervert!"

Suddenly, Mrs. Snyder appeared in the doorway to Ruthie's room. She was holding a big, black iron frying pan in one hand.

"So what's all the screaming," she inquired while looking at me suspiciously. I jumped up from the bed. Nothing particularly clever came to mind.

"Hello, Mrs. Snyder, what do I smell cooking in the kitchen?"

"Nothing's cooking. So why all the hollering? What's wrong?" she asked, seeing nothing wrong but sensing some mischief was afoot.

"Nothing's wrong. I was just leaving, that's all."

I squeezed past her, smiling my best smile and saying, "I'll see myself out. Don't bother."

Then, with an inexplicable display of adolescent bravado, I called back over my shoulder, "See you tomorrow, Ruthie. Hope you'll be feeling better!"

After my hasty retreat from Ruthie's bedroom, I knew that if there was going to be any explaining to do, it would have to come from Ruthie.

****

Although my friends were of slightly different ages, we all graduated from Boys High in 1943. In less than a year each of us was destined to ride the West End subway to his appointment with a recruiting officer of the United States armed forces. Jake was bigger and a few months older than the rest of us, and was the first to sign up. As a long-time Eagle Scout, he felt compelled to join the marines. One by one the guys all disappeared from the block. Zahn enlisted and after completing basic training was sent to O.C.S. When Bernie finished basic he joined the ski troops, thinking he'd go skiing in the Swiss Alps or something. Sandy wound up in the 7th Army as a radio man. Everybody went except me. I wasn't seventeen yet and had to wait until June rolled around before I was old enough to enlist in the Air Force.

While I waited I grew lonely. There was no one left to play stick ball or hand ball with me. Even looking in on Ruthie at night didn't seem as much fun alone as when the guys were with me. Rita and Gloria tried to cheer me up, but it did no good. I missed the guys. Finally, on my seventeenth birthday, I rushed off to war. I guess I must have thought it would be fun and games. After three years of military service, the B-25 I was in crashed on landing and my shoulder was smashed to pieces. In a very short time I was home, discharged from the U.S.A.A.F.

I was the first to return to 50th street. It was 1946 and before the year was out, all the guys had returned home. Except for Jake. Jake was killed on a beachhead somewhere in the Pacific. So we sat on our dead friend's stoop and shot the breeze. Bernie told us how the ski troops had slogged their way up the boot of Italy, always deep in mud without a snowflake in sight.

Some of his toes became gangrenous and had to be amputated. Zahn told us how he led a patrol with the 3rd Division; how they chased the German army from hedge-row to hedge--row until he had been hit by a sniper's bullet which broke his left femur in half and blew out most of his thigh muscles. I suppose by telling each other war stories we were purging our souls of khaki covered memories. Sandy, however, did not join us in shooting the breeze. He would never get to see the Grand Tetons like Jake, but he never said a word about how he had been blinded. And we didn't ask. We could see the scars.

One Saturday night, for no reason I can remember, we all decided to put on our uniforms and assorted ribbons and check out the girls along Flatbush Avenue, the shopping center of Flatbush. When no pretty girls could be found, we wound up at Perry's Bar over on McDonald Avenue under the old Culver line tracks. Perry's was the only bar for miles. Jake always used to say that the trouble with Borough Park was that it had too many synagogues and not enough bars. Before long we were deep into the spirit of the night. Bernie stood up and proposed a toast to Jake.

"We're drinkin' tonight to the end of our friend. His life was nothing special except it was too damn short."

Bernie looked up at the ceiling and raised his glass.

"Hear me O Zeus, Jehovah, and whatever Goddamn gods may be... and let Jake Goodman beat the ass off all those other dead Jews from Brooklyn in that great stick ball game in the sky."

He lifted his drink, said L'chaim, and emptied his glass.

"L'chaim," we all repeated.

We were pretty well sloshed by the time we got around to singing our old school song.

"Here's to Boys High, grand old Boys High, Here's to all her loyal men on field and track, Here's her banner, a glori..."

I interrupted the singing to ask if any one of us had ever received a letter from one of the girls on the block while we were overseas.

"Let's see. I think I got two letters from Rita while I was chasing Germans across France," Zahn said. "She confessed her undying love for me and how much she missed my Groucho imitations."

Bernie said, "A letter from Gloria caught up with me while I was in a hospital in Rome. She wrote that she would always love me like a brother, but was presently going out with an officer in the navy. Did great things for my morale."

It was Sandy's turn. "I got Ruthie's letter just before I got hit. The 3rd Division had been pushing the Germans for weeks and..." his voice trailed off.

He paused as if he were unsure of his memories or uncertain whether he wanted to confide in us. We all knew that he had been a radio man with the Seventh Army when it broke through the Siegfried Line.

"Go on, Sandy," I said. "We're listening."

Very quietly, in a steady monotone, Sandy resumed his war story. He said his outfit had been under a mortar barrage for hours. A shell had exploded in front of him, blowing him into a mortar hole. Shrapnel had torn away part of his face, splintering his eyes with shards of steel. He had done the best he could to stanch the blood, sprinkling sulfur powder over his wounds and bandaging his bleeding eyes. The worst part was the medics couldn't get to him. The whole night he lay in his hole hoping the Germans would continue to retreat so the medics could find him in the morning. When they finally did reach him he was taken to a field station, patched up, transfused, and then flown to England where plastic surgeons tried to put his face back together. Unfortunately, the doctors couldn't do much about his eyes.

"Tell me," said Bernie, "while you were lying in that lousy mortar hole all through the night, what were you thinking about?"

"The truth?"

"Yeah, the truth!"

"Ruthie. I thought a lot about Ruthie."

"You thought about Ruthie? Why you dirty minded son-of-a-bitch, what you really mean is you thought about Ruthie's pair. Tell the truth! Ruthie's breasts danced inside your head like sugar plums. Right?"

Very softly Sandy responded. "Yeah, I guess maybe you're right. That and other things."

For some obscure reason, I looked at my watch. It was nearing 11:30, Ruthie's time of night. As one man we rose from the table of discarded bottles and empty glasses, accidentally knocking over Sandy's cane. We left Perry's Bar and piled into my old '36 Buick. In less than ten minutes we disembarked on 50th Street, between 15th and 16th Avenues. Standing in front of Jake's stone stoop where we once played a high stakes game of stoop ball, we surveyed the terrain.

No black-coated, long-bearded enemy forces were observed to be lurking about. We slipped into the shadows of Jake's driveway and made our way across the open ground of two back yards until we came upon our objective.

Ruthie's rear window was lit and the shade was drawn. Bernie was dispatched to the Ilex bushes and quickly returned with our faithful old milk box, a little more rusty perhaps, but serviceable nevertheless. Zahn was the first to take up our favorite observation post, his nose pressed to the sill, eyes squinting against the light. Anxiously, we waited turns.

Of course, the question uppermost in everyone's mind was whether time's horny-fingered hand had diminished the stalwart beauty of Ruthie's heroic pair. Perhaps too many indiscretions with guys loose on furlough, or perhaps…"Fantastic!" Zahn held out his hands and shook them.

"Incredible!" Bernie nodded his head in mock disbelief.

I got up on the milk box and looked in. An old lady in a floral patterned, flannel housecoat was regarding herself in the dresser mirror. She slowly moved her hands up to the top of her head and began picking pins out of her hair. She removed a large chignon and placed it in a glass jar on the dresser.

"Well, what do you think?"

Sandy was standing so close to me that even in the dark I could see the patchy skin of his plastic face. What was the truth about Ruthie's memorable pair? Surely, wherever she was, her breasts were magnificent still.

"Well, what do you think?" Sandy repeated the question.

I got off the milk box and put my hands on his broad shoulders.

"You want to know what I think. I think…"

Before I could finish what I was going to say, a loud strident voice rang out in the darkness of the driveway.

"Hey, you guys, what do you think you're doing? You crazy or something?"

I stared past Sandy into the shadows, trying to discern who it was that had called out. Then I recognized Freddie, Zahn's kid brother, grown a whole lot bigger and a lot louder.

"Don't you guys know the Snyders moved away? Ruthie doesn't live there anymore!"

I could feel Sandy expel a long, slow breath. I took my hands off his shoulders, put one arm around his waist, and guided him back to the street where we all once lived and played.

Court Martial at Sheppard Field

Ross Seymour and his luscious, sexy date arrived at the main gate to Sheppard Field just in time for the U.S.O. dance. The guard at the gate looked into the back seat of the cab and recognized Ross.

"You're outa luck Ross, there's a riot goin' on in Hangar One and all MP's are ordered to check in and get their gear. You better get your ass over to the Provost-Marshal's quarters right quick."

Ross knew that instead of getting laid that night, he was getting screwed by the fuckin' army. Regretfully, Ross told the cab driver to take the overly ripe Mary Jean home. Then, still wearing the class A uniform he had decked himself out in, and still smelling from the strongly aromatic bay rum aftershave lotion he had applied so profusely, he headed directly to Hangar One to see what the hell was going on. From the main gate to the flight line the road was as straight as an arrow. It didn't take him long to get there.

The first thing he saw inside the hangar was Hot Lips Page up on the bandstand. The man was blowing The Star Spangled Banner out of his horn as loudly as it could possibly be trumpeted at the same time his band was blasting away. But the plain truth was that no one was paying much attention. What Ross saw going on around him was a race riot in full swing. White guys were swinging at black guys, black guys were swinging at white guys. Women were screaming.

Up on the track which ran around the second tier of the hangar, soldiers were feeding coins into a Coca Cola machine and throwing the green bottles down into the crowd below. As each bottle hit the cement floor it exploded like a fragmentation grenade. Shards of glass flew off in all directions. One piece of glass cut Ross across his face. He put his handkerchief up to his cheek and saw blood on it. He cursed the Air Force for making him an MP They had taken one look at his infantry service record and seen that his M.O.S. (Military Occupation Specialty) was Rifleman. They probably figured a guy with that kind of training would make a good MP Of course, they never asked him what he thought. Ross looked around again at what was going on. Any idiot could figure out what had happened to start the riot. Hot Lips Page and his men were a black band. The soldiers at the dance were white men and black men, not used to mingling with each other in America's segregated army. Even their barracks were separated from each other at opposite ends of Sheppard Field. Hell, they didn't even eat together in the big mess hall.

And without a doubt, the big bad fly in the ointment was the fact that the officer in charge of festivities had simply forgotten to invite the ladies from the black U.S.O. in the hardscrabble town of Wichita Falls. Then, when the music began and the couples took to the floor, an enterprising black soldier from a city up North had cut in on a white soldier from a city down South. "May I have this dance, ma'am..."

Ross had seen enough. What the hell did the Air Force expect him to do? He was damn sure he was not going to use his club on one of these guys and get himself killed in the process. He let himself out a door at the back of the hangar.

The next day Ross was lying on top of his cot reading a copy of Stars and Stripes when a Lieutenant stuck his head into the barracks.

"Hey Ross, it's show time. We got trouble with the black guys again. Report to the Provost-Marshal's office on the double. That's an order!"

Ross thought about yesterday's riot in Hangar One. He didn't want any part of that again. Nevertheless, he put on his gear which consisted mainly of stiff canvas puttees, a wide canvas cartridge belt, his sidearm, a heavy wooden baton, and his white helmet liner with a big black MP stenciled on its front. Then he jogged down to the Provost building which also served as headquarters for the military police. It wasn't far. When he got there he saw other MP's shaping up.

He was issued the familiar M-1 and a clip. Ross stared in disbelief at the clip of eight shiny 30 caliber bullets. In the past, whenever he took German and Italian prisoners of war out on a work detail he was given a rifle, but no clip, no bullets. The first time that he was responsible for such a detail of prisoners he asked the sergeant who had handed him the M-1 why there was no ammunition. The soldier looked at him like he was nuts.

"What the hell do you think you need ammo for? These P.O.W.'s are the happiest men in this man's army. The war is over for them. They eat the same food we do, they wear the same clothes we do, and for all I know, they fuck the same U.S.O. dames we do. And anyway, where they gonna run to? This is Texas. A couple hundred miles in any direction don't make no difference, there's nothin'. Forget about it. You don't need no bullets."

Ross inserted the clip into the chamber of the M-1 and went outside to see what was happening. The first thing he saw was a Lieutenant lining up some MP's. The officer saw Ross and motioned to him. He fell in with seven other MP's. In the best military tradition, the First Lieutenant said, "Follow me." And off they went down the wide street that ran from the flight line to the main gate.

After just a few minutes, Ross saw the rioting men coming towards them. The Lieutenant leading the MP's called for them to halt. He drew them up in a line across the road and told them to assume the position of parade rest. Ross had a moment to study this officer. He was bronzed from the Texas sun. His pale blue eyes were bland and devoid of expression. He had a chest filled with ribbons. Ross made out the European Theater, a Purple Heart, a Bronze Star, and...God only knew what all the other ribbons stood for. Pinned above them all was a pair of silver wings.

"Men, I'm going out to meet these colored boys to see what their problem is. You stay here and listen for my orders. I'll be telling you what to do."

Ross sensed a deep confidence born from experience in the man's slow southern drawl. Then the Lieutenant turned and walked up the road to meet the oncoming soldiers. Ross noticed that this handsome figure of a man walked with a slight limp.

The black soldiers were something scary to see. Ross guessed that they were a hundred strong. Maybe more. They marched toward the line of MP's four and five abreast. Some wore fatigues, some wore class A's, others were stripped to the waist. Many were swinging baseball bats and waving cue sticks taken from recreation barracks. And worst of all they were chanting loudly, "WE WANT BLACK! WHITE BITCHES NO! WE WANT BLACK! WHITE BITCHES GO!"

Standing no more than ten yards from the oncoming mob, the southern Lieutenant held up his right hand. The soldiers in the front ranks came to a stop. Then the Lieutenant took a few steps backward and drew a line in the dust that was always blowing across the road. Ross heard his brief speech.

"Now boys, I want you to listen to me very carefully because your lives may depend on what I say. I want you to look back there at my men. You see they have rifles. They are prepared to use them when I give the signal. So here is what I'm telling you. Go back to your barracks. Go back and tell your captain what your problem is. I'm sure the Air Force can work this thing out so y'all be made happy. Now that's all I'm going to say. The rest is up to you. Take my advice and go back. Now!"

The Lieutenant calmly turned his back on the black soldiers and walked over to the line of MP's. He directed his men to fire the first round over the heads of the angry soldiers when he gave the command. Ross suddenly realized that this was not a game. This was not training camp. The brave Lieutenant was at war. This was combat for him. And he knew combat. Ross watched as the Lieutenant slowly returned to the spot where he had drawn a line in the sand. Not five minutes had gone by. But it was enough time for Ross to think. He knew deep in his heart that he could not use his weapon against these men. He had gone to Boys High School in Brooklyn with guys like these. He had played basketball with them. Many thought of him as a friend. Now he could see that the black soldiers were arguing among themselves. Ross' anxiety increased. He prayed the men would return to their quarters and avoid a confrontation. They didn't.

Suddenly, and all together, they strode forward descending upon the line of MP's. Ross heard the Lieutenant's commands as from a great distance.

"READY!"

Seven M-1's pointed skyward.

"AIM!"

Seven M-1's swung down.

"FIAAH!"

The sound of the volley from seven rifles tore through the Texas air like the sound of a pneumatic jackhammer. POOM . . . PUHPOOM . . . PUHPOOM . . . POOM . . . POOM. The black soldiers standing at the front broke ranks at the first sounds of the discharge. They turned in panic and fell over the men immediately behind them. They dropped their bats and sticks in their desperation to get away from the line of fire. Their panic spread rapidly and in a matter of seconds all the men could be seen running back up the road toward the safety of their barracks. Without question, the rebellion of the black soldiers at Sheppard Field was over.

"Mister, you didn't fire your piece!"

The southern Lieutenant with all the ribbons on his chest and the bland blue eyes was standing directly in front of Ross. Ross, to his everlasting sorrow, was still standing at parade rest. He had never made any motion to raise his rifle.

"Let me see your tags," the officer ordered.

Ross reached inside his fatigues and handed the metal tags, still on their chain, to the Lieutenant, who studied the dog tags for a moment and then asked Ross, "Are you of the Hebrew persuasion?"

The question surprised Ross.

"Yes, sir."

The officer's handsome face did not change expression.

"Who is your commanding officer?" the Lieutenant asked.

"Foxx, sir. Captain Leonard Foxx," Ross answered.

"I know him, a good officer," said the

Lieutenant. "You report back to him and tell him that I'm placing you under house arrest until a court-martial can be held. You disobeyed a direct order. You understand? You hear what I'm saying?"

"Yes, sir."

"Well, don't just stand there. Get going."

Then the southern officer turned to the other MP's who were still standing at parade rest and dismissed them saying, "Y'all did good; we sure showed them colored boys a thing or two. I'm proud of you."

The MPs quickly dispersed. On the way back to his company area Ross felt sick to his stomach. He realized that he was absolutely scared stiff of what might happen if he were to be court-martialed. He sought out Captain Foxx and found him holed up in a little office he had made for himself at the end of one of the company's barracks. It was hot and cramped inside. Ross wasted no words in telling the Captain what had happened on the main road as he and seven other MP's faced the rioting black soldiers. He finished by telling Foxx the southern Lieutenant had threatened him with a court-martial for failing to fire his rifle.

Captain Foxx listened patiently to Ross without interrupting him. Then he took Ross outside and offered him a cigarette. Both men lit up.

"Looks like we got trouble, right here in River City," the Captain said.

"It's not funny," Ross replied. "This is fuckin' Wichita Falls, Texas and that Lieutenant with all those ribbons on his chest sure meant business. He wasn't just foolin' around. I'm scared stiff."

"Well, you shouldn't let this shit get to you. I'm sure I can figure something out. You can count on me."

Immediately, the Captain's words made Ross feel a whole lot better. He had always liked Foxx and now he loved him.

"You go back to your barracks and sit tight. Try to show a little confidence. I'm pretty sure I'll come up with something."

For the next three days Ross remained in his barracks and worried himself sick as he contemplated being court-martialed. Then the order he feared would come finally arrived. In it he was told to report to the office of the Provost-Marshal to stand trial.

Captain Foxx accompanied him on the way over and told him what his defense should be and what he must say to the hearing officer. The Captain's instructions made a whole lot of sense to Ross because they really described what he was feeling when ordered to fire a big fat 30 caliber bullet over the heads of the rioting soldiers. It turned out that the hearing officer was the Provost-Marshal himself, a full Colonel.

"Corporal Seymour, I have your complete military history in this file in front of me. I see from it that you have been in service three years and have never gotten into any kind of trouble before. I also see that your M.O.S. is that of an infantry rifleman. Now I want you to please tell this court why you refused to obey a direct order to fire your rifle when ordered to do so by Lieutenant Conners."

Captain Foxx had anticipated just such a question and had drilled Ross on what he must say in order to refute the charge against him.

"Colonel, sir, after thirteen weeks of basic training my unit was required to go through a night infiltration course. Watching tracers from the machine gun emplacements ricochet off rocks that were not in their line of fire, I learned what a short round was. And there were more than a few that fell short. I also went through the German village where we fired our rifles at plywood figures painted to look like German soldiers."

Ross could see that the Colonel was growing impatient with this recital of his military history.

"Corporal, get to the point you are trying to make!"

"The point is, sir, that all through my infantry training I thought I was being prepared to fight German soldiers. It never occurred to me that the first time I was ordered to fire my rifle it would be to shoot at American soldiers."

The Colonel looked at Ross for what seemed to be an eternity. It was impossible to read the expression on his face. When he finally spoke Ross trembled at the thought of what his decision might be.

"After investigating the purported misbehavior of a few colored soldiers on the street that leads from the main gate to the flight line, I find that there is insufficient evidence to support the charge against Corporal Ross Seymour of failing to obey a direct order from a superior officer. Therefore, as the Provost-Marshal of Sheppard Field and acting in my official capacity, I consider it my duty to summarily dismiss any and all charges against Corporal Seymour in this matter. Furthermore, I order that he be returned to active duty immediately. Let it be so noted in the record of these proceedings."

Without further ado the Provost-Marshal rose from his seat and left the room.

Outside the courtroom, Captain Leonard Foxx shook a Lucky out of its pack and put it in his mouth. He shook out another and gave it to Ross. Then he lit both cigarettes with a silver Zippo lighter. Both men inhaled deeply.

"Captain Foxx," said Ross, "I think this is the beginning of a beautiful friendship."

The Marcolini Effect

Ross was assigned to New Utrecht High School in the fall of 1952 as a teacher of Art. New Utrecht served the boys and girls of Bensonhurst, a section of Brooklyn that was primarily, mainly, and almost completely Italian. One afternoon at the end of the school day as Ross was entering his parked car, he was accosted by three boys in black leather jackets.

"Hey teach, you got a cigarette?"

Ross, wishing to appear friendly, offered each of the boys a Lucky. The tallest of the three, his cigarette dangling from his mouth, stuck his face in Ross' face and said,

"Light it!"

There could be no mistaking the insolent challenge in the dark eyes staring into his. Ross quickly realized that his response to this confrontation would determine his status as a new teacher at New Utrecht, as well as his personal reputation in the neighborhood. Pushing the young man away with his open hand, Ross said,

"Light your own fuckin' cigarette!"

Then he turned his back on the three of them and tried to get into his car. Big mistake! A hand gripping his shoulder quickly spun him around and a fistful of bare knuckles exploded in his face. The initial blow was followed by a torrent of punches to his face and stomach, delivered by all three boys. Ross fell to the ground, his briefcase spilling its contents onto the sidewalk. All the fight had gone out of him when the first punch had smashed his nose and caused his eyes to tear up. He could taste the blood in his mouth from a split lip.

But the worst happened next. The boys attacked his beautifully restored '39 Chevy. They broke off the antenna, they kicked in the front grill, they took a nail and ran it down the length of the car, cutting through the paint and exposing raw steel. Then they sauntered off down 80th street, arm in arm, laughing as they went, as proud of the assault as if they were the three musketeers.

Ross picked himself up and drove home. His apartment was in a two family house that was only ten minutes away from the school.

He parked the car in front of the house and walked toward the steps that led to his front door. Standing in the pathway to his front door was his landlord, Al Mazzini.

"Hey, Ross, what happened to you? Your face looks like it was pushed through a meat grinder."

Ross saw no way of avoiding the truth, so he told Al about his encounter with the three boys who had beaten the living daylights out of him. The expression on Al's face changed to one that was terrible to behold. He looked as if someone had just told him that a gang of Puerto Ricans had broken into his house and robbed him. Ross already knew that Bensonhurst was a town filled with more than its share of ethnic prejudice.

Nevertheless, it's important to understand the kind of man Al Mazzini was. Al was a longshoreman. When Ross first met him standing in front of his house, Al was wearing a sleeveless undershirt and a pair of dirty jeans. Hanging from his side on a black leather belt was a big longshoreman's hook – a very mean-looking piece of equipment that seemed to be a permanent part of Al. Moreover, it was quite apparent that he was endowed with huge muscles. His biceps alone were the size of Ross' calf muscles and the girth of his chest and back was pure Superman. There could be no doubt that working on the docks moving heavy crates from ship to shore and shore to ship for twenty-odd years had made Al the strong man that other men in the neighborhood respected. His reaction to Ross' story of the one-sided fight was simple and to the point.

"You want I should fix it for you?"

"Gee, Al, would you do that for me?"

"Sure, not a problem."

Immediately the two men hatched a plot. They agreed that on the next Friday at three o'clock, Ross would follow Alfano, Romano, and Marcolini from the school building. He would point out the boys to Mazzini, who would be waiting in his parked car in front of the high school on 16th Avenue.

That Friday, when the three boys turned the corner on to 80th Street, Mazzini's big Cadillac also turned the corner and slowly followed them. Ross noticed that another man was seated next to Al.

A week went by. There was no sign of Alfano, Romano, or Marcolini in or around New Utrecht High School. Ross began to worry.

"Hey, Al, what did you do with those boys? I haven't seen any of them in school."

"You don't have to worry, Ross, I just talked to them. That's all."

"You just talked to them?"

"Yeah, it's like I said, I just talked to them."

Almost two weeks went by when, as if summoned by the spirit of Utrecht itself, all three boys walked into Ross' classroom. Their attitude had apparently undergone a major tectonic shift. Without being given instructions of any kind, they busied themselves restoring the painting set-ups on all the desks. That task included dumping the dirty water from thirty large tin cans, refilling the cans with clean water, and washing the bristles of all the paint brushes. The boys repeated this procedure in all of the art classes. During the actual class time the three of them had the good sense to disappear into the halls of the school.

There were other strange developments. The young men began bringing Ross stolen property to store in his closet. They brought him four hubcaps from a new Cadillac. Cadillac hubcaps were considered a highly desirable prize in Bensonhurst. Boxes of brand new Champion spark plugs materialized on his desk. Ross had no idea what they would bring him next. He ordered them to stop or he promised to call the cops.

Then, on a day he would never forget, Ross was standing in the hall outside his art room when he witnessed an ugly little tableau vivant. There was Marcolini, his arms pumping his fists like pistons against the stomach of a big kid whose back was up against a wall of the building. Finally, Marcolini delivered a powerful punch to the face which sent the teen-ager to the floor, where he lay crumpled up, sobbing in pain. Then Ross saw Marcolini put his arm around the shoulder of a small boy who had been standing nearby and walk with him down the hall.

As they passed by, Ross heard Marcolini say to the kid, "Well, I'm pretty sure Pugliese ain't gonna bother you no more. And by the way, here's your lunch money. I took it back from him when I beat him up."

Ross watched as Marcolini handed a couple of bucks to the kid.

The next time Ross saw Marcolini he asked him who the little kid was for whom he had stood up in bloody combat. He looked at Ross with a blank face.

"You know, the little kid you returned the lunch money to."

"Oh, you mean Lil' Joey. He's my friend Romano's kid brother. I've known him just about all my life."

This simple statement gave Ross pause for thought. When he returned to his classroom and sat down at his desk, a new portrait of Marcolini's character was created in his mind. Marcolini was being transformed into the Knight of the Black Leather Jacket, a sworn protector of little kids, a dedicated defender of the innocent. Hmmm. What if he were to employ Marcolini as a kind of amanuensis? Instead of *writing* what he dictated, Marcolini could *enforce* what he dictated.

The more he thought about it, the more persuasive the idea became to him. Ross was certain Marcolini would willingly get involved if he were to be given the role of defender of academia, the first law of which was: "Discipline, Discipline, Discipline."

Ross didn't have long to wait to try out his most unconventional strategy. Only a few days after the notion had first occurred to him a student used insulting language to express his sharp disapproval of Ross and his teaching methodology. Ross warned him to stop his invective, but the young man persisted in his abuse. Ross could not allow himself to be vilified in such a manner in front of the other students. When the bell rang ending the class, Ross located Marcolini and dictated the first of what would become many disciplinary assignments. Not only did he name the offending student, but he took considerable time to explain the reason for the mission.

At the end of the day, as the boy was crossing the schoolyard on his way home, he encountered Marcolini, who politely asked him if he knew what behavior was required of him in the art room. The kid mumbled a smart-alecky reply, to which Marcolini responded by beating him to a pulp. After three or four similar disciplinary meetings between misguided students and Marcolini, news got around New Utrecht High School that some sort of a connection seemed to exist between Marcolini's actions in the schoolyard and a student's behavior in Ross' art room.

Later in the same school year a fearsome brawl broke out in the schoolyard. Louder than usual, dozens of boys from New Utrecht were fighting with a gang of boys from Fort Hamilton High School. New Utrecht girls were screaming at the top of their lungs. Someone called the police. When the cops arrived in their black and white cruisers, they immediately set about dispersing the boys with nightsticks, while pulling and pushing some of them into their patrol cars. All of this was observed by Ross and other teachers who had left the building to see what the commotion was all about.

Back in school, after spending hours at the local precinct, Marcolini sought out Ross to ask a question that had been troubling him for some time. Familiar with Ross' schedule, Marcolini waited until Ross had a free period. Then he marched into the classroom to spill what was on his mind. He wanted to know why the cops always picked on him. He said there were a lot of guys involved in the fighting but the cops never failed to single him out and throw him into a police car and take him down to the station house.

Ross studied Marcolini, trying to see what the cops saw when they looked at him. Marcolini was bigger than most young men his age. He was broad shouldered and at seventeen he possessed the muscular development of a mature man. Ross also knew that the bold gaze of his dark eyes could be interpreted as being insolent and challenging. Another feature which stood out and appeared to be Marcolini's pride and joy was the shock of thick black hair that covered his ears and the nape of his neck, and which he habitually seemed to be combing up into a pompadour. In addition, Ross was acutely aware of the fact that along with Marcolini's ever-present comb he carried a switch blade. It seemed to be de rigueur for all the guys at New Utrecht to carry a comb and knife. It was as if they considered these two items to be standard equipment along with their notebooks and ballpoint pens.

However, when a big fight erupted and police arrived at the scene of the turmoil, the guys would surreptitiously pass the knives to their girlfriends, who stood in back of the crowd which had gathered to watch the action. There seemed to be some kind of tacit understanding between the guys and the police in which the police never frisked the girls when they searched for concealed weapons.

Nevertheless, when all the factors contributing to the behavior of the police were considered, Ross knew that it wasn't Marcolini's physical attributes that were the cause of the police picking him out of a group of guys whenever a street fight was in progress. Indeed, Ross had a very clear idea of the dynamics involved in these confrontations. Three years of duty as an MP in the United States Army had taught him a thing or two about street fights between rival platoons and police actions aimed at controlling out-of-control men.

Then and there, Ross told Marcolini that he would have to change his appearance if he wanted to avoid being arrested.

"What do you mean, change my appearance? I can't change who I am!"

Ross saw that Marcolini was woefully upset. He tried to explain what he meant.

"You know those black leather jackets you and Alfano and Romano are always wearing?"

"Yeah? What about 'em?"

"Well, have you ever given any thought to the signal those jackets send to the police?"

Marcolini looked perplexed. Ross made an effort to clarify what he was driving at.

"Look, I'll try to be clear. You have to understand what I'm saying. Those black jackets scream at the cops: 'Here I am, look at me, I'm a tough guy, a smart-ass from the streets of Bensonhurst, so whatch'ya gonna do about it?' See what I mean?"

A faint smile spread across Marcolini's handsome face as he listened. It was plain to Ross that the young man had finally caught on to how the game of cops and teen-age tough guys was played.

"You mean to tell me that something as stupid as a leather jacket makes the goddamned police single me out as some kind of criminal?"

"Yes, that is exactly what I'm saying."

It was at that very moment that Ross was inspired by the idea of a dress code.

"Marcolini, my lad, what you need is a disguise, and I'm going to show you how to get one."

But first they had to get some money. To that end Marcolini accompanied Ross on a trip to his mother's house. Once there, Ross told Mrs. Marcolini what he had in mind. He explained why it had become necessary for Frankie to change his appearance in order for him to acquire protection from the minions of the law. After listening to Ross for a few minutes, Mrs. Marcolini proclaimed her son's undying innocence in all things relating to the police. She informed Ross that her Frankie was an angel who always helped her with the shopping and scrubbed the floors on the weekends.

Then Mrs. Marcolini asked Ross to follow her into the kitchen. On a shelf in the kitchen was a jar in which she kept dried basil leaves. She reached into the jar and pulled out a loose bunch of ten and twenty dollar bills. She counted out one hundred dollars and handed it to Ross.

"Now go take care of my Frankie."

Thus fortified with cash, Ross and Marcolini got into Ross' old Chevy, picked up Marcolini's pretty girlfriend Terry at her house, and drove to Macy's on Flatbush Avenue. Once in the men's department it didn't take long to buy five white shirts neck size 17, sleeve length 34, and five imported silk ties. Terry helped Marcolini pick out the ties which she thought to be most attractive. They also bought a brass tie clip with a big letter 'M' at its center. To put it in 1950's parlance, both Terry and Frankie thought the clip to be the 'cat's meow.'

Then they drove back to the Marcolini household to show Mrs. Marcolini their purchases and to return the money they had not spent. One hundred dollars went a long way in the 50's.

Much to their surprise, Mrs. Marcolini was not entirely pleased. She wanted to know why Ross had not gotten a sport jacket for her Frankie, such a handsome boy. She gave him some more money so he could buy a good one. They had no choice but to drive back to Macy's. This time, Ross made sure that the young man's disguise was complete. He had him try on a camel-hair blazer, which Marcolini immediately fell in love with.

During the week that followed, Ross taught Marcolini how to tie a silk tie into a broad Windsor knot. He also took him to his favorite barber shop where tonsorial artistry was performed on Marcolini's thick crop of long black hair.

Finally on a Sunday afternoon, Frank Marcolini put on one of his new shirts and ties, tied the tie into a Windsor knot, combed his shortened hair three times, put on his new jacket, stood in front of his mother and Terry and asked,

"How do I look?"

Mrs. Marcolini nodded her head in approval and kissed her son on the forehead.

Terry said, "Frankie, you look like a million bucks!"

Later that day, when Ross saw the sartorial splendor of Marcolini, he knew beyond a shadow of a doubt that no officer of the law would dare lay a finger on him ... no way.

Back at New Utrecht High, whenever Marcolini was carrying out a mission for Ross in the schoolyard, he would carefully take off his camel-hair blazer, hand it to Romano or Alfano for safe keeping, and then proceed to beat the stuffing out of some kid who had earned Ross' opprobrium. Students at New Utrecht were quick to see that although Marcolini had inexplicably altered his appearance, he most definitely had not changed his personality.

After a few more years spent at New Utrecht, Ross passed the New York City Board of Education's examination for becoming an English teacher. That next September he was assigned to Sheepshead Bay High School where he taught for ten more years. Nevertheless, his new teaching role and his new assignment did not affect the nature of his relationship with Marcolini. That continued unabated. Whenever a student at Sheepshead demonstrated disrespect in the classroom or gave him a hard time in some unruly manner, Ross would avail himself of Marcolini's most effective services. It was not long before all of his English classes were under picture-perfect control. Discipline was no longer a matter of concern for Ross.

Upon occasion Ross would overhear other teachers in the cafeteria commenting upon and wondering about the excellent behavior of the students in his classes. For his part Ross ignored them, never responding to their open admiration of what appeared to be his exceptional teaching ability.

The years rolled by. One day Marcolini met Ross outside Sheepshead in order to confide in him and tell him what was happening in his life. Marcolini told Ross that his uncle Antony had lost his household moving business and had been forced to sell his two trucks. Ever since graduating from New Utrecht, Marcolini had worked for his uncle moving furniture in and out of houses. Now, as a result of Antony losing his business, Marcolini found himself unemployed and with nothing to do. So he had come to Ross to ask him his opinion of a new job opportunity he had been offered.

Marcolini said a guy had come to his house when his mother was not home and had asked him to join a local organization. He also said that the guy told him he could make a lot of money if he became a member.

"What's the name of this organization?" Ross asked.

Marcolini smiled sheepishly, looked down at the sidewalk, hesitated a moment, and then said

"Murder Incorporated."

Ross was not surprised. He knew that many a young man from Bensonhurst nursed a secret ambition to become connected to one mob or another.

"How come he came to you?" Ross asked.

"He said that I was recommended by someone in the neighborhood."

"Listen to me Frankie. I don't think you really want to become a murderer. Do you?"

There was no response from Marcolini so Ross continued. "Those guys at Murder are not like you. They kill people. They use guns to get their way. They're nothing but a bunch of well-dressed cowards. I know you. You're not like them. You're a born street fighter. You use your fists to get your way. I repeat. You're not like them. Don't let them persuade you with their lies about big money. They will only use you and in the end they will probably get you killed. So don't be a fool. Tell them they can all go to hell."

Marcolini listened but remained prophetically silent. Ross knew that somehow he would have to do more if he wanted to dissuade the gullible young man from becoming a gangster and possibly a murderer.

The summer came and went. Ross transferred from Sheepshead Bay High School to Midwood High School in Flatbush. And then, close to the end of the year, fate unexpectedly stepped in to take a hand in helping Ross solve what he had come to think of as the "Marcolini dilemma."

The unforeseen event for which he had been hoping appeared in the form of the Daily News, its pages spread out on a table in the teacher's lounge. A modest headline on page 4 announced in bold face type:

United States Post Office Schedules Examination for Postal Employees

Ross went on to read that mail carriers were needed in many of Brooklyn's districts. He wasted no time in notifying Marcolini about the coming exams. Ross promised Marcolini that he would help him study whatever it was the Post Office required him to know.

Marcolini seemed interested and Ross, true to this word, helped him prepare for the examination. He was gratified when Marcolini passed and became a regular mailman with a daily route in Bensonhurst. It turned out that Marcolini loved his job. He loved the fact that all the people in the neighborhood recognized him and said hello to him. He considered himself lucky to be a mailman.

As for Ross, well, after thirty years he finally retired from teaching. He had a big retirement dinner at Fortunato's Ristorante on 5th Avenue in Bensonhurst. Teachers came from New Utrecht, Sheepshead Bay, and Midwood, from all the high schools where he once had taught. After dinner, when he was handed a microphone and asked to say a few words, he thanked his old colleagues for taking the time to come to his party.

Then a principal he had known at Sheepshead Bay called out, "Hey, Ross, tell us what your secret was. I'm sure everybody here would like to know how you were able to control those lousy kids in your classes. We all know your kids acted as if they were little dolls. C'mon, tell us how you did it, the discipline I mean?"

Ross hesitated to tell the teachers gathered there what he knew to be the truth about himself and the way in which his classroom discipline had been obtained. Then he figured what the hell, what have I got to be afraid of? I'm retired now. But as Ross was about to reveal the nature of his secret alliance with Marcolini, he suddenly experienced a strong disinclination to speak about it. What was there about his relationship with Marcolini that was appropriate for him to now reveal? Hadn't Marcolini served him loyally all those years when he needed him? Was he now going to disclose what he did and why he did it? After all, who was he, Ross, to impugn the reputation of a United States Postal employee who walked the streets of Bensonhurst every day of his life delivering the mail?

He began his remarks by saying, "I'm sorry to have to tell you this, but there was no secret. There was no magic wand. I was just a regular teacher like the rest of you. Every weekend I'd go home and spend hours writing out lesson plans for the coming week. I simply tried to design lessons as interesting to my students as I could possibly make them. As for the discipline you observed in my classes and have asked me about, I haven't a clue why my kids behaved so well. I guess they just loved me."

Three Stones for Rebecca

Sam began talking about visiting Rebecca early in August. He was sitting at our dining room table on a Saturday night, loudly eating the dinner his daughter had prepared for him. Without looking up from his food, the old man began talking to the boiled chicken on his plate.

"I got a cousin Stevie – you should meet him someday – who flies with his family all the way down from Cleveland so he should visit with his mother in her grave. It costs him a lot of money; he should do this to show some respect for the dead."

Ross and his wife exchanged glances. They recognized Sam's words as the opening remarks of what they had come to regard as the Rosh Hashanah talk. Every year for twelve years, when Rosh Hashanah came around, Sam visited Rebecca's grave. He was following a tradition observed by Jews for over two thousand years, to go on a pilgrimage to the graves of their loved ones at the coming of the New Year.

The next weekend, after the customary Friday night meal, it was raining hard and Ross drove his father-in-law home. Alone in the car with his daughter's husband, Sam seized the opportunity to express his thoughts.

"So tell me Ross, have you visited your father in his grave yet?"

Ross was silent and gave no reply.

"Such a good man. Do you remember what a good man he was and how much he loved you? So tell me honestly, would saying a little prayer hurt so much?"

Ross thought of his father's fatal heart attack and ached with the pain that returned at the memory of it.

By the end of August, Sam was more direct with both of them.

"A little visit. What is it? It's the only thing we can do for her…now. You remember how much she did for us?" And finally, "I'm an old man. Who knows how much longer I've got. I may not live 'til September." Sam coughed.

It was a bit too much. Then Sam informed his daughter Livia that he was planning on taking a taxi out to the cemetery.

"It's only a four hour trip. Not such a big deal!"

Livia felt an immediate sense of guilt.

"Ross, we have to go. I can't allow a sick old man to travel so far alone."

Ross hated the idea of the trip and the heavy traffic he knew they were sure to encounter. Woodlawn Cemetery, after all, was located at the far end of the Long Island peninsula. Nevertheless, he also knew that it was time to go.

Early in the morning of the first Sunday in September, they set out on the long trip to the cemetery. Almost four-and-a-half hours later they passed through the wrought iron gates of the cemetery and pulled up in front of the white administration building. A man wearing a shabby blue serge suit and a frizzled gray beard was standing alone at the bottom step of the building. He held a small black book in one hand.

Ross knew that the man had taken up his solitary position on the stair in order to be asked to perform the services of a rabbi. By reciting the Hebrew prayers for the dead he would be giving solace to a mourner and, at the same time, the mourner would be performing a 'mitzvah' by retaining the man in the threadbare suit for a small sum of money.

Ross watched as his father-in-law struggled to lift his arthritic body out of the car. Black cane coaxing the ground for support of each tentative step, Sam slowly approached the man with the frizzled beard and shabby suit. They exchanged a few subdued words, the stranger nodded his head, and together they walked back to the car. The bearded one helped Sam into the rear seat next to Livia and then got in on the passenger side next to Ross. Ross started the car and in just a few minutes they arrived at that section of the cemetery where Rebecca lay buried.

Since Sam now experienced difficulty reading from the tiny Hebrew text in the prayer book, he merely listened as the man in the shabby suit raised his voice to heaven and exhorted Jehovah to provide an eternity of peace to the beautiful soul of the woman who lay at his feet. Sam tried to join in the chanting of the ancient Hebrew words, but his voice was feeble and repeatedly broke under the strain of his grief. Red-eyed and tearful, he leaned heavily on his daughter's arm, and mutely stared at the blank half of the granite headstone upon which his own epitaph would someday be engraved.

Finally, the bearded rabbi stopped his chanting, closed his little prayer book, and signaled that the religious ritual was done. Still holding onto his daughter's arm for balance, Sam stooped over and picked a small stone from among the pebbles strewn around the graveside. Straightening up, Sam placed the stone on a corner of Rebecca's headstone. Ross and Livia did the same, each placing a stone next to the one Sam had left. Three small stones now rested atop Rebecca's headstone.

Driving away from the grave, Ross noticed that small stones lay on the tops of many of the monuments in the cemetery. Arriving back at the administration building, Sam extended his arm to shake the rabbi's hand, all the while thanking him for the excellent service he had provided. As the man with the frizzled beard and shabby, blue serge suit opened the door of the car, Ross held him with a question.

"Rabbi," Ross deliberately chose the term to show his respect, "what is the religious significance of the little stones we placed on Rebecca's headstone?"

The man thought a moment and said, "That's only a custom, a thing people do to show that they have visited the grave. Nothing else."

The man then closed the car door and stuck his bearded face into the open window as if to give special emphasis to his words. "As for its religious significance...there is none. No significance at all!"

Ross just stared at him. A bearded man in a tattered suit. Somehow Ross found him irritating. Without saying another word, he gunned the engine and headed the car out onto the highway.

As he drove home, the image of the three stones resting on Rebecca's headstone stuck in his mind. Rebecca was in his mind. He was remembering her. She was a gentle woman. In Russia she had been a nurse. He had pictures of her in a white uniform with a red cape. During the early years of his marriage, he had lived in her house where she had always shown him nothing but kindness and consideration. When he dislocated his shoulder her strong fingers massaged his muscles until they grew hot and he felt the pain go away. When his first son was born she crooned to the baby while she changed his diapers. Ross smiled as he recalled her telling him to always keep his fingernails clean.

"Why Rebecca? Why is it important that I keep my nails clean?"

"Because," she said, "you use your hands when you make love to my Livia." Oh, Rebecca, Rebecca, you're too much!" And Ross kissed her on the cheek. Through the years he learned to love her.

As Ross continued driving down the highway, he thought about the three small stones again. He was pretty sure he knew what they stood for. Their meaning was clear to him.

Made in the USA
Charleston, SC
24 March 2014